Chloe

charmz™

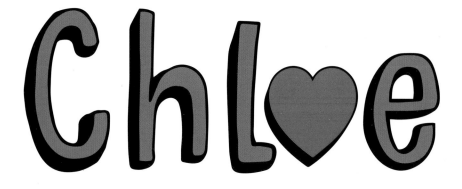

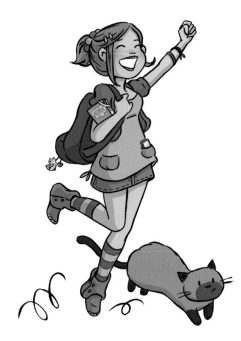

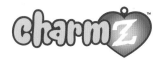

Chl♥e

Story by Greg Tessier
Art by Amandine

NEW YORK

Thanks to you—you're not dreaming, no, no!—and to you over there, too—don't hide, don't be shy! And to you, too, of course, how could I forget you? In short, thanks to all those who were able to awaken my curiosity and who will certainly recognize themselves in these few lines.
—Greg

Thanks to my incredible support group (Drac, Sam, David, Yaooo and Tomatias!) Thank you to Mom and Dad, for your encouragement and advice! Thanks, too, to ZouZou for the first read-through along with Fleurette in the bedroom in Villeneuve! Thanks to Greg for having the idea for this awesome collaboration! And an especially big thanks to Pierre, the charming young man from the office next door, without whom this book would be very bland!
—Amandine

Mistinguette [CHLOE] volume 1 "En quête d'amour" © Jungle! 2011 and
Mistinguette [CHLOE] volume 2 "Baisers et coquillages" © Jungle! 2012
Jungle!, Miss Jungle! and the Jungle! logo are ®2017 Steinkis Groupe
www.editions-jungle.com. All rights reserved.
Used under license.

English translation and all other material © 2017 by Charmz.

CHLOE #1
"The New Girl"

GREG TESSIER and AMANDINE — Story
AMANDINE — Art and color
AMANDINE — Cover
JOE JOHNSON — Translation
SASHA KIMIATEK — Production Coordinator
DAWN GUZZO — Diary page design
JEFF WHITMAN — Assistant Managing Editor
RACHEL GLUCKSTERN, GREG LOCKARD — Orginal Editors
MARIAH MCCOURT — Editor
JIM SALICRUP
Editor-in-Chief

Charmz is an imprint of Papercutz.

ISBN HC: 978-1-62991-772-6
ISBN PB: 978-1-62991-763-4

Printed in China
May 2017

Charmz books may be purchased for business or promotional use.
For information on bulk purchases please contact Macmillan
Corporate and Premium Sales Department at (800) 221-7945 x5442

Distributed by Macmillan
First Charmz Printing

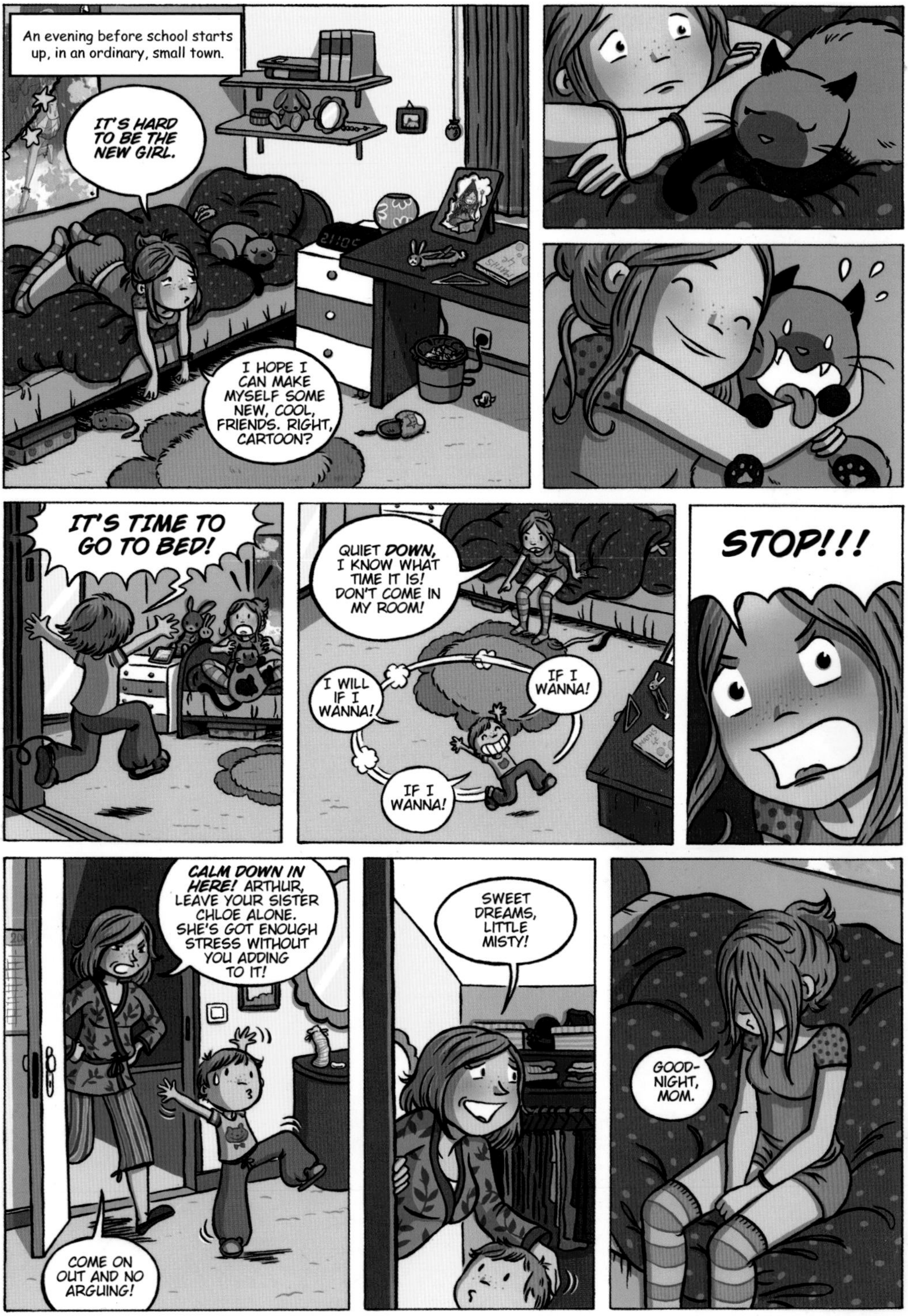

An evening before school starts up, in an ordinary, small town.
IT'S HARD TO BE THE NEW GIRL.
I HOPE I CAN MAKE MYSELF SOME NEW, COOL, FRIENDS. RIGHT, CARTOON?
IT'S TIME TO GO TO BED!
QUIET DOWN, I KNOW WHAT TIME IT IS! DON'T COME IN MY ROOM!
I WILL IF I WANNA!
IF I WANNA!
IF I WANNA!
STOP!!!
CALM DOWN IN HERE! ARTHUR, LEAVE YOUR SISTER CHLOE ALONE. SHE'S GOT ENOUGH STRESS WITHOUT YOU ADDING TO IT!
COME ON OUT AND NO ARGUING!
SWEET DREAMS, LITTLE MISTY!
GOOD-NIGHT, MOM.

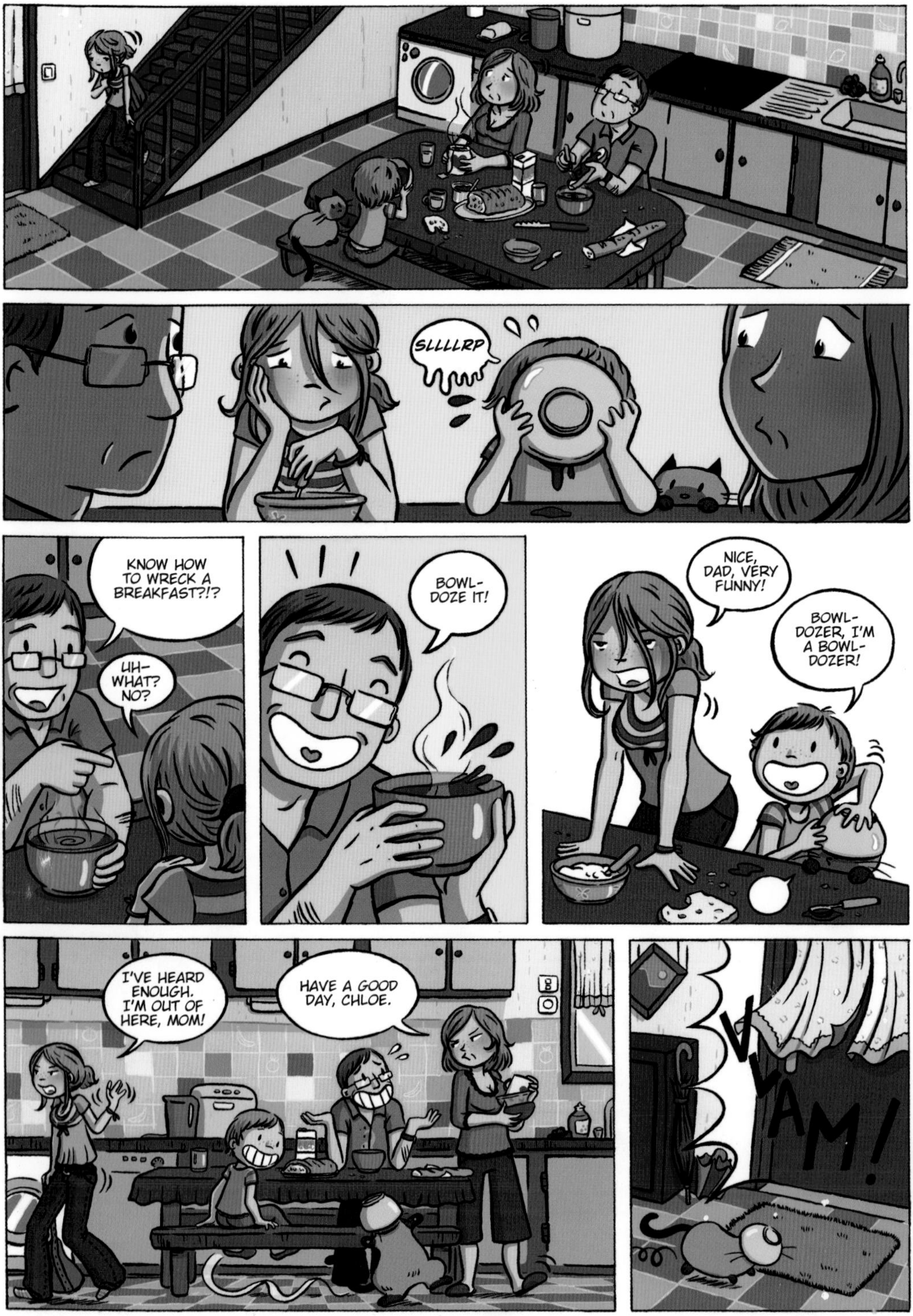
SLLLLRP
KNOW HOW TO WRECK A BREAKFAST?!?
UH-WHAT? NO?
BOWL-DOZE IT!
NICE, DAD, VERY FUNNY!
BOWL-DOZER, I'M A BOWL-DOZER!
I'VE HEARD ENOUGH. I'M OUT OF HERE, MOM!
HAVE A GOOD DAY, CHLOE.
VLAM!

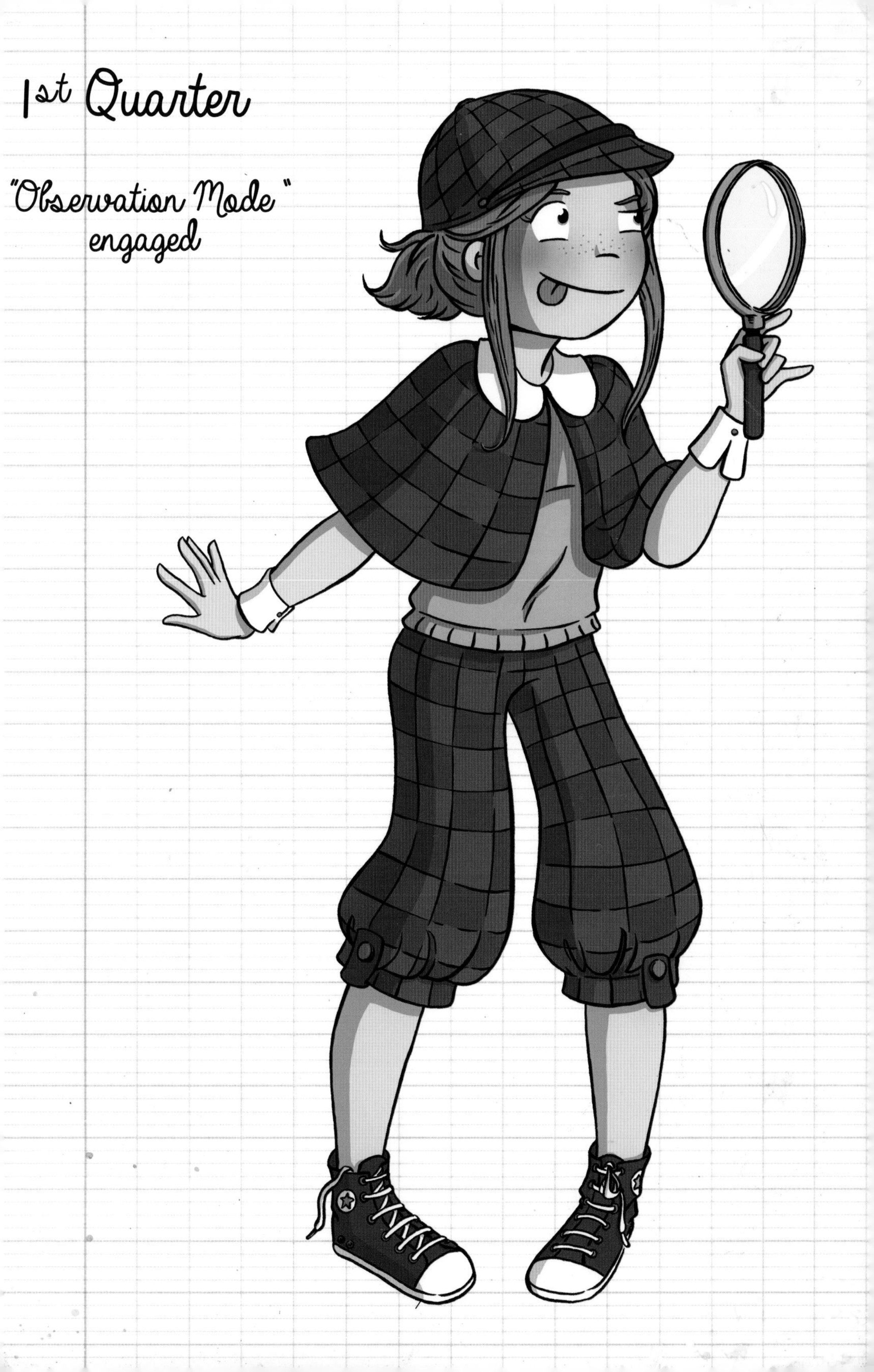
1st Quarter
"Observation Mode"
engaged

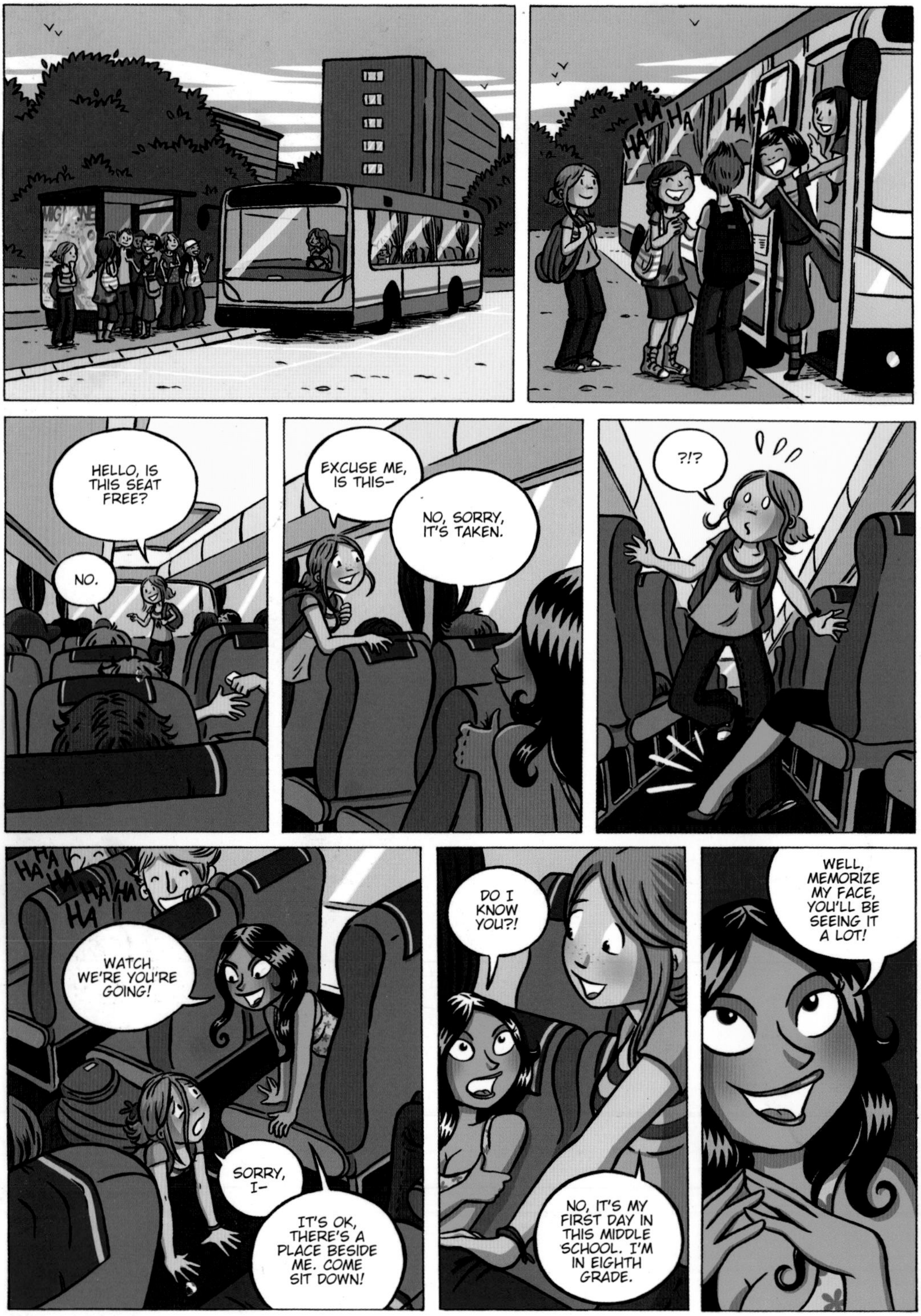
HA HA
HA HA
HELLO, IS THIS SEAT FREE?
NO.
EXCUSE ME, IS THIS–
NO, SORRY, IT'S TAKEN.
?!?
HA HA HA HA HA
WATCH WE'RE YOU'RE GOING!
SORRY, I–
IT'S OK, THERE'S A PLACE BESIDE ME. COME SIT DOWN!
DO I KNOW YOU?!
NO, IT'S MY FIRST DAY IN THIS MIDDLE SCHOOL. I'M IN EIGHTH GRADE.
WELL, MEMORIZE MY FACE, YOU'LL BE SEEING IT A LOT!

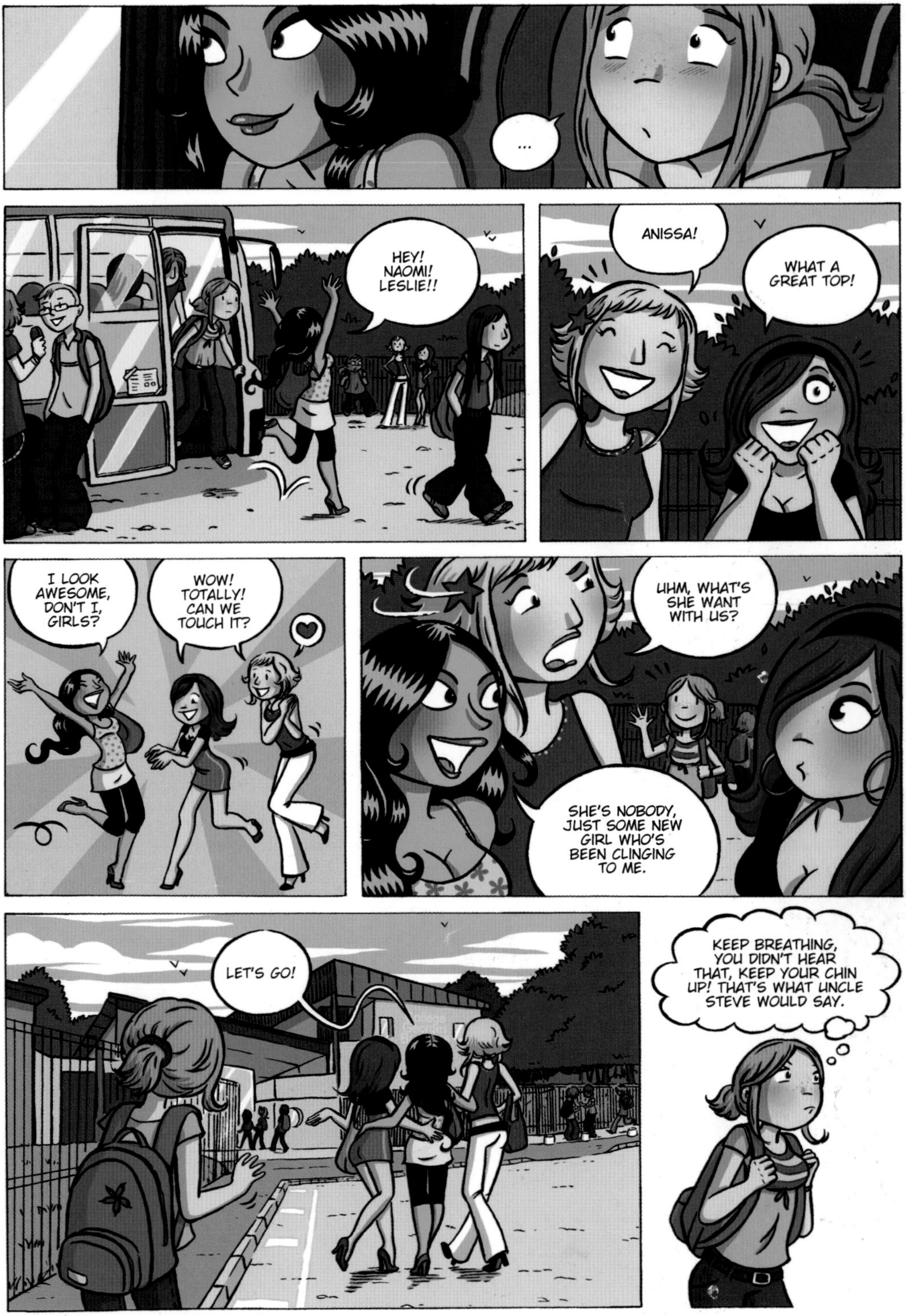
...
HEY! NAOMI! LESLIE!!
ANISSA!
WHAT A GREAT TOP!
I LOOK AWESOME, DON'T I, GIRLS?
WOW! TOTALLY! CAN WE TOUCH IT?
UHM, WHAT'S SHE WANT WITH US?
SHE'S NOBODY, JUST SOME NEW GIRL WHO'S BEEN CLINGING TO ME.
LET'S GO!
KEEP BREATHING, YOU DIDN'T HEAR THAT, KEEP YOUR CHIN UP! THAT'S WHAT UNCLE STEVE WOULD SAY.

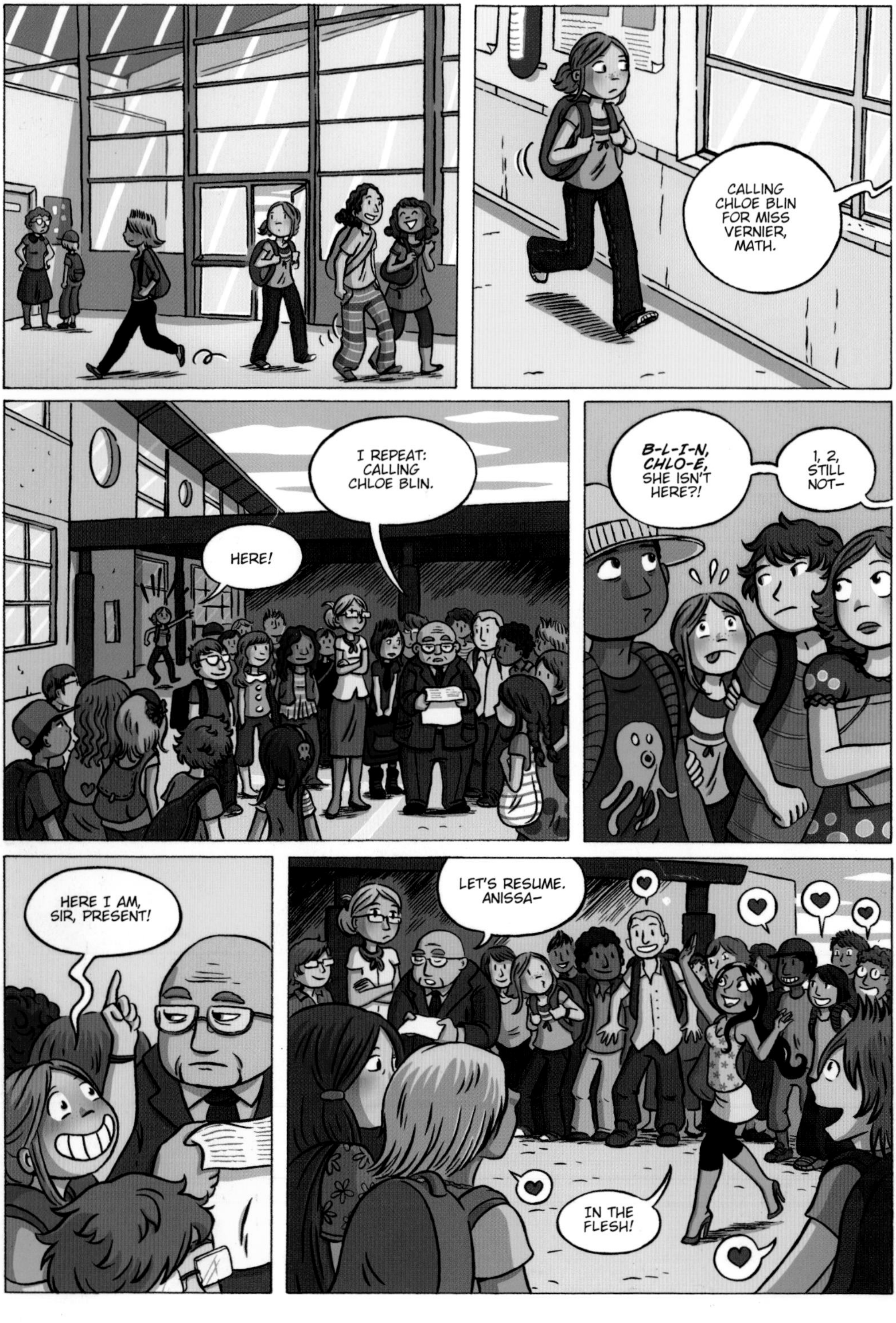
CALLING CHLOE BLIN FOR MISS VERNIER, MATH.
I REPEAT: CALLING CHLOE BLIN.
HERE!
B-L-I-N, CHLO-E, SHE ISN'T HERE?!
1, 2, STILL NOT-
HERE I AM, SIR, PRESENT!
LET'S RESUME. ANISSA-
IN THE FLESH!

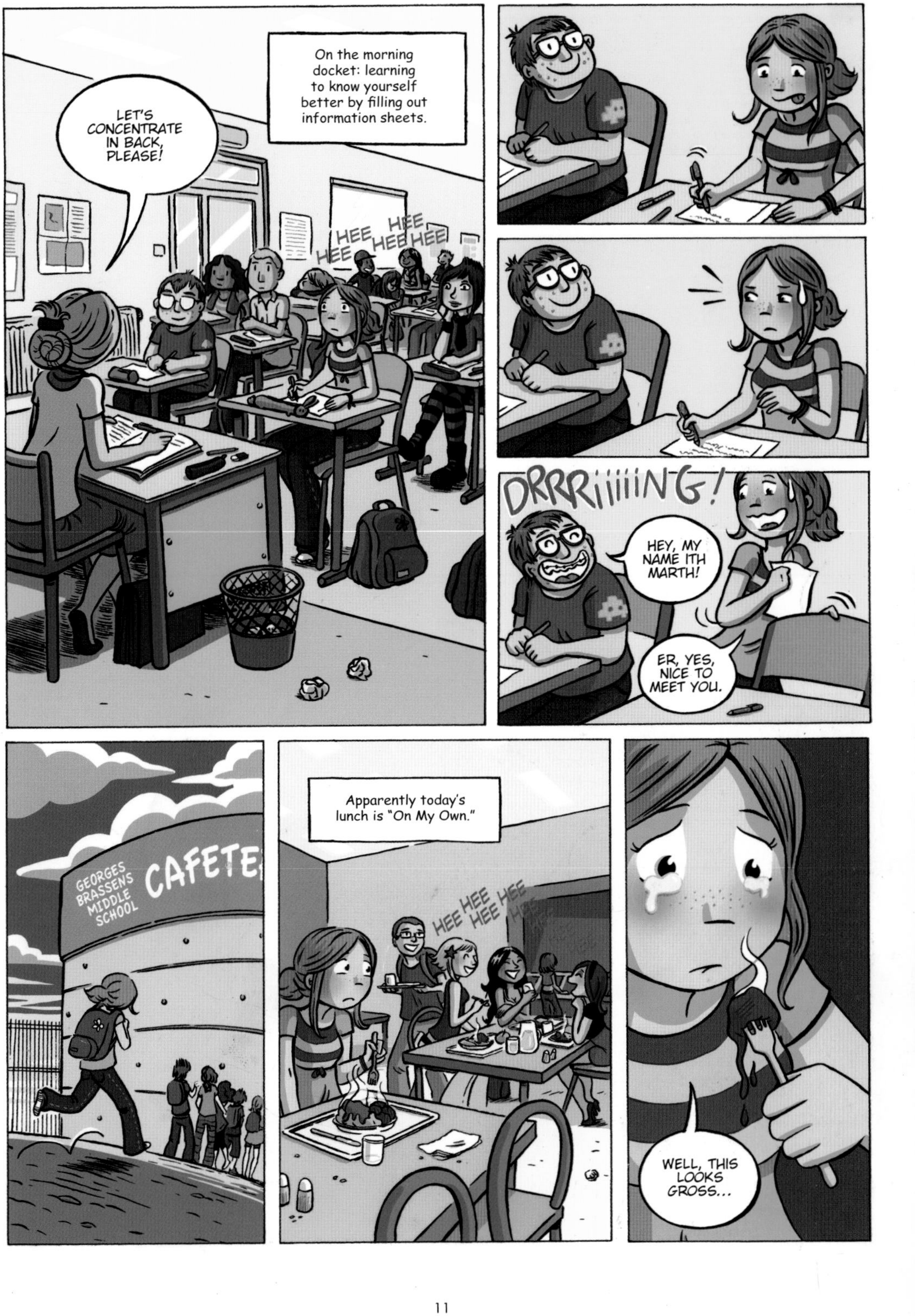

On the morning docket: learning to know yourself better by filling out information sheets.
LET'S CONCENTRATE IN BACK, PLEASE!
HEE HEE HEE HEE HEE
DRRRiiiiiNG!
HEY, MY NAME ITH MARTH!
ER, YES, NICE TO MEET YOU.
GEORGES BRASSENS MIDDLE SCHOOL
CAFETE
Apparently today's lunch is "On My Own."
HEE HEE HEE HEE
WELL, THIS LOOKS GROSS...

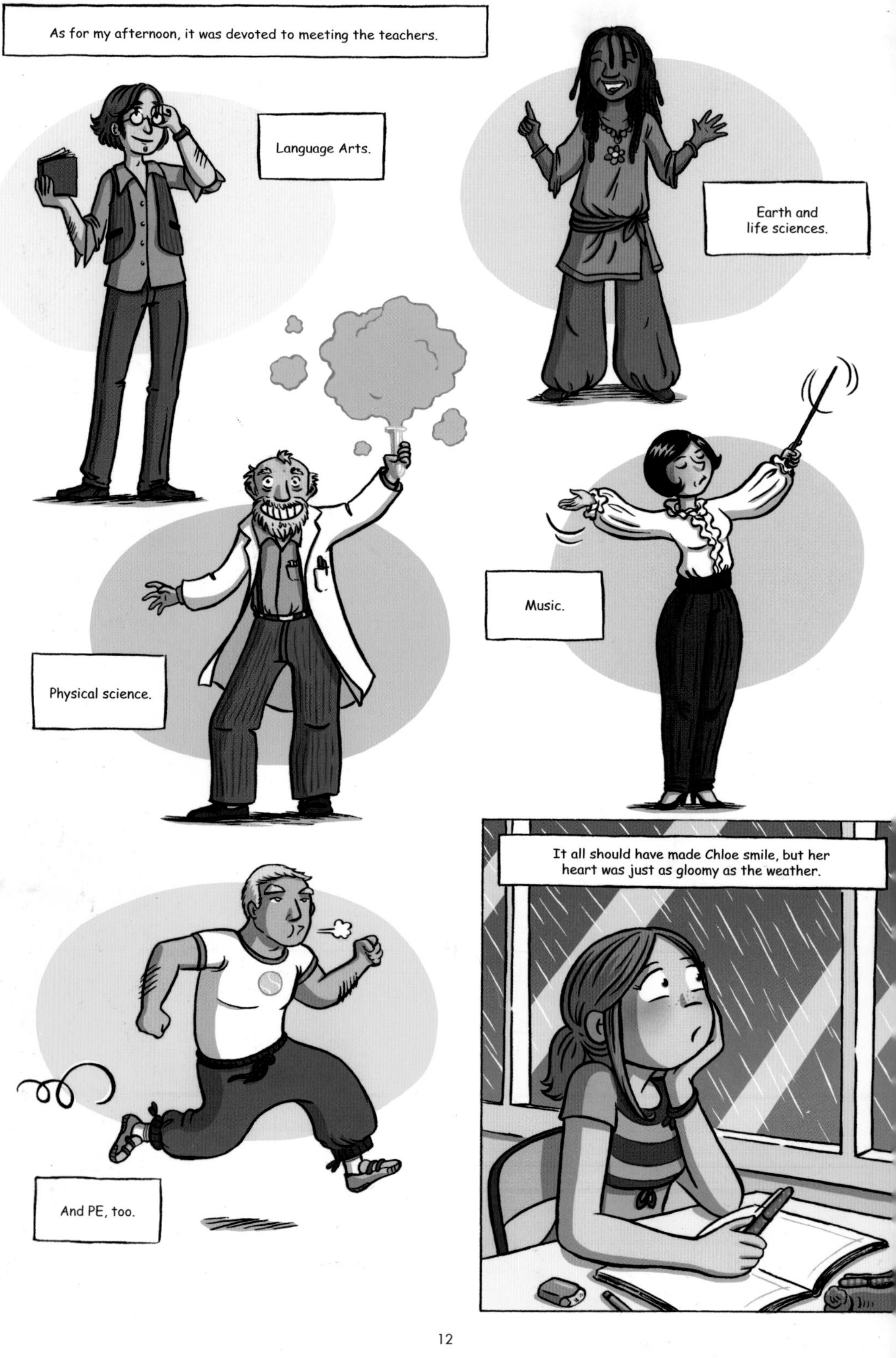
As for my afternoon, it was devoted to meeting the teachers.
Language Arts.
Earth and life sciences.
Physical science.
Music.
And PE, too.
It all should have made Chloe smile, but her heart was just as gloomy as the weather.

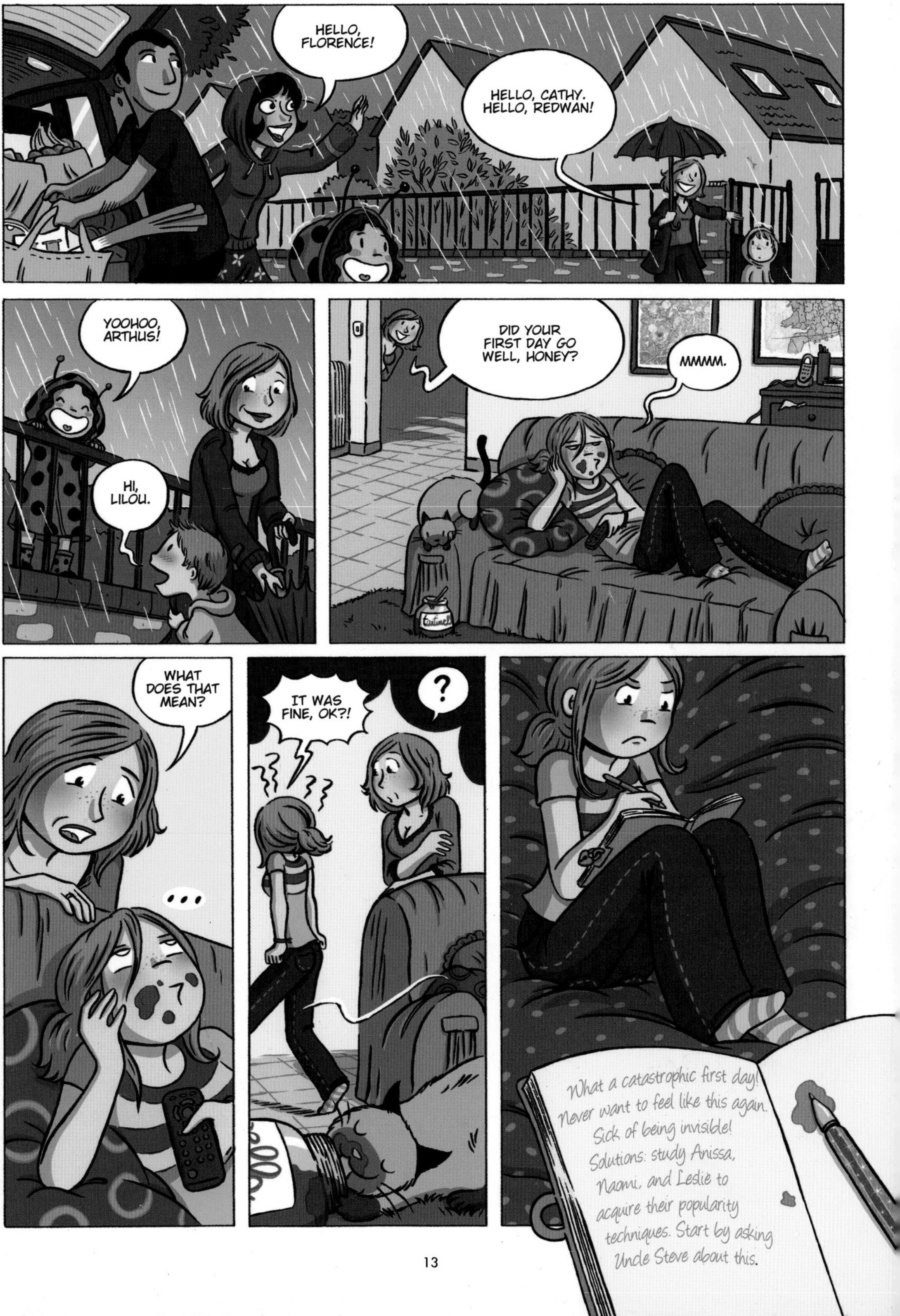
HELLO, FLORENCE!
HELLO, CATHY. HELLO, REDWAN!
YOOHOO, ARTHUS!
HI, LILOU.
DID YOUR FIRST DAY GO WELL, HONEY?
MMMM.
WHAT DOES THAT MEAN?
...
IT WAS FINE, OK?!
?
What a catastrophic first day!
Never want to feel like this again.
Sick of being invisible!
Solutions: study Anissa, Naomi, and Leslie to acquire their popularity techniques. Start by asking Uncle Steve about this.

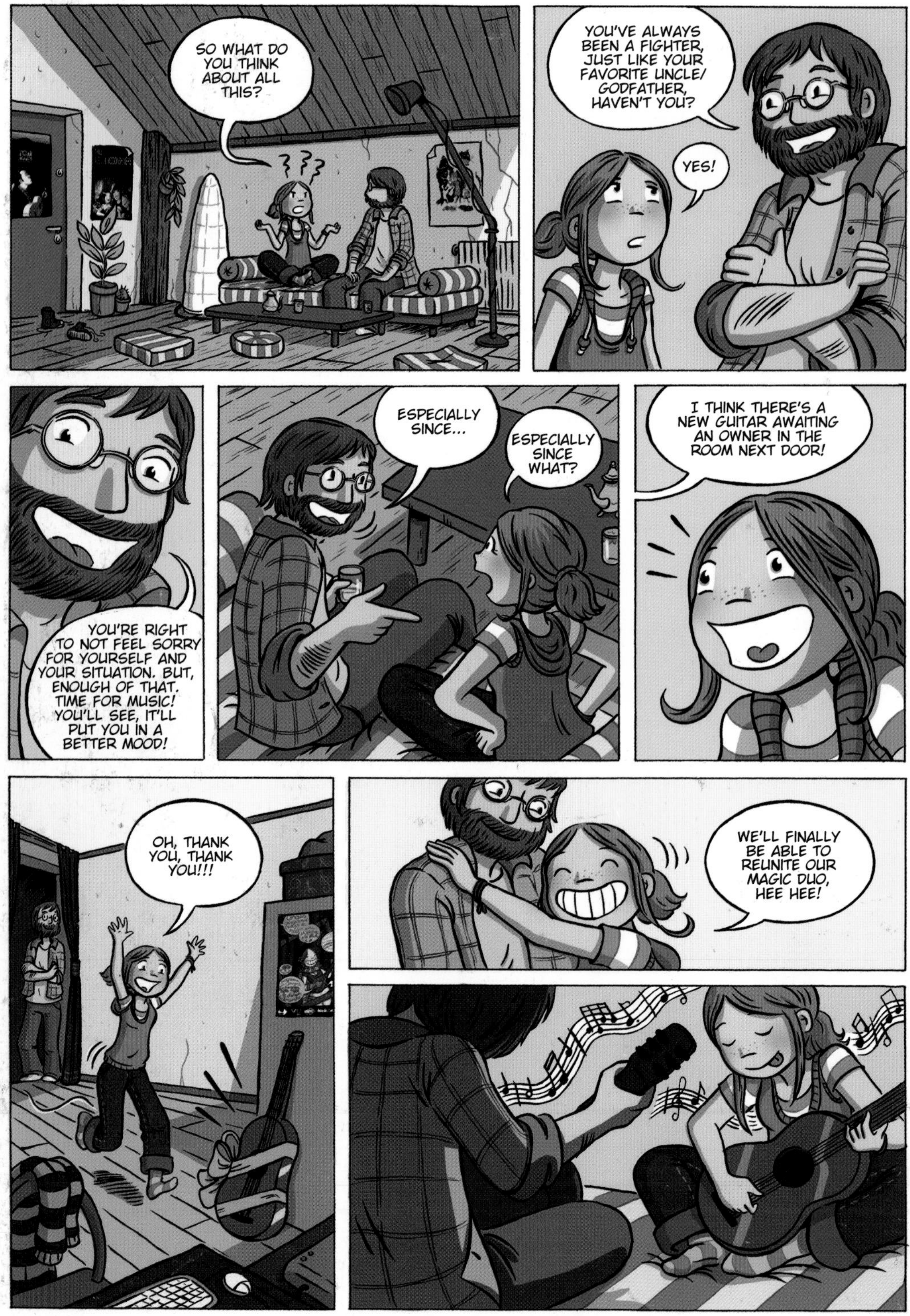
SO WHAT DO YOU THINK ABOUT ALL THIS?
YOU'VE ALWAYS BEEN A FIGHTER, JUST LIKE YOUR FAVORITE UNCLE/ GODFATHER, HAVEN'T YOU?
YES!
YOU'RE RIGHT TO NOT FEEL SORRY FOR YOURSELF AND YOUR SITUATION. BUT, ENOUGH OF THAT. TIME FOR MUSIC! YOU'LL SEE, IT'LL PUT YOU IN A BETTER MOOD!
ESPECIALLY SINCE...
ESPECIALLY SINCE WHAT?
I THINK THERE'S A NEW GUITAR AWAITING AN OWNER IN THE ROOM NEXT DOOR!
OH, THANK YOU, THANK YOU!!!
WE'LL FINALLY BE ABLE TO REUNITE OUR MAGIC DUO, HEE HEE!

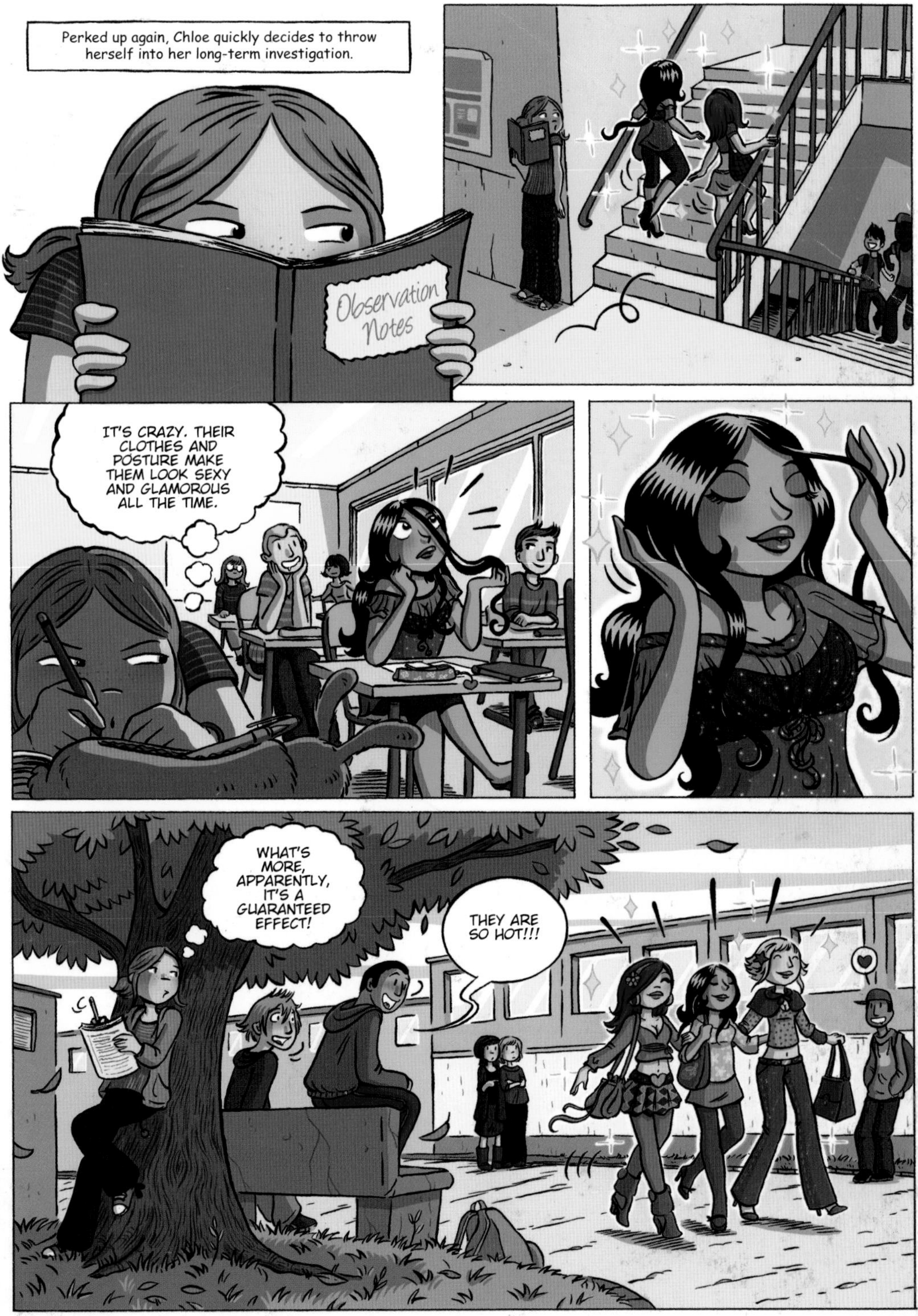
Perked up again, Chloe quickly decides to throw herself into her long-term investigation.
Observation Notes
IT'S CRAZY. THEIR CLOTHES AND POSTURE MAKE THEM LOOK SEXY AND GLAMOROUS ALL THE TIME.
WHAT'S MORE, APPARENTLY, IT'S A GUARANTEED EFFECT!
THEY ARE SO HOT!!!

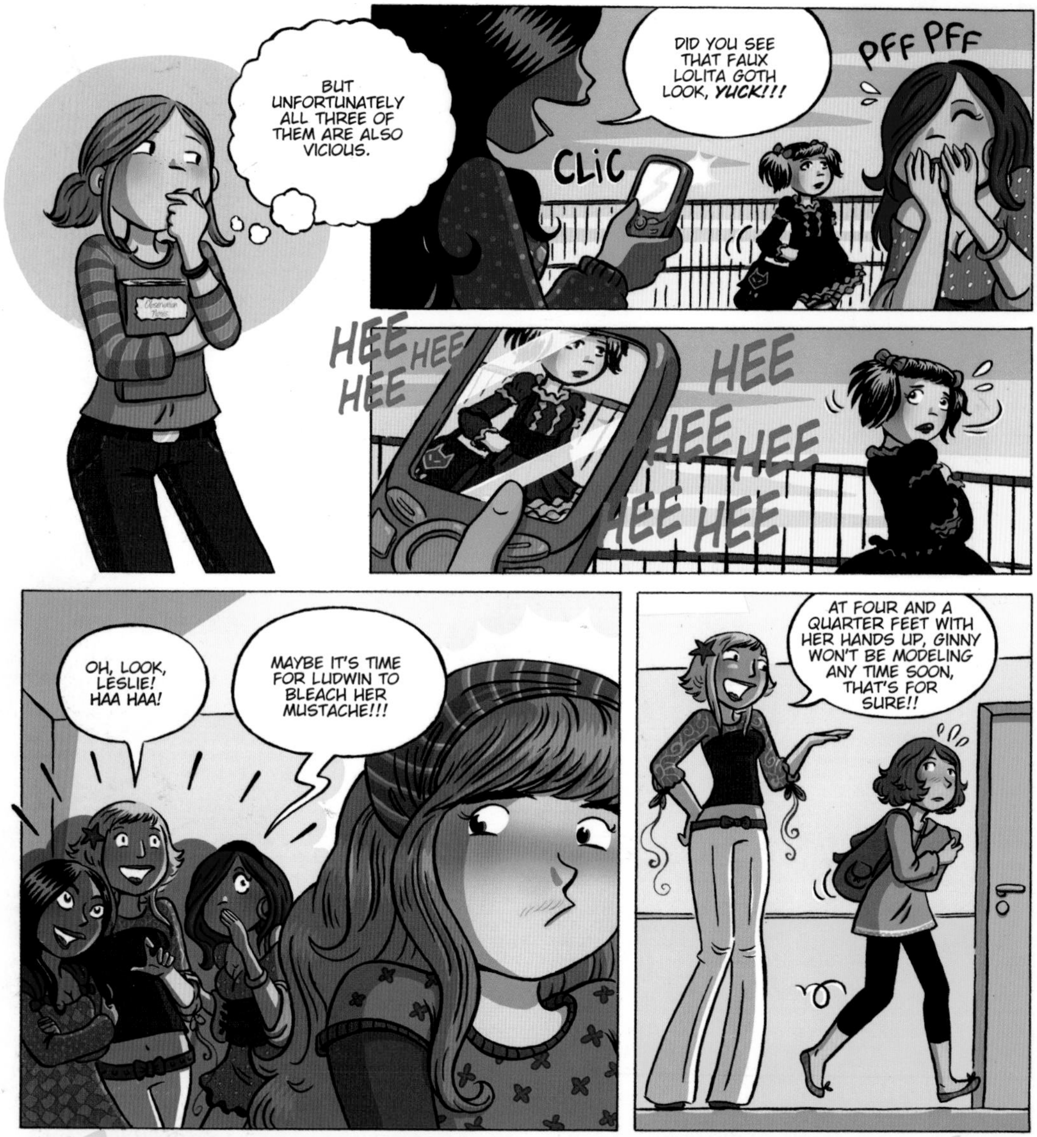
BUT UNFORTUNATELY ALL THREE OF THEM ARE ALSO VICIOUS.
DID YOU SEE THAT FAUX LOLITA GOTH LOOK, YUCK!!!
PFF PFF
CLIC
HEE HEE HEE
HEE HEE HEE HEE HEE
OH, LOOK, LESLIE! HAA HAA!
MAYBE IT'S TIME FOR LUDWIN TO BLEACH HER MUSTACHE!!!
AT FOUR AND A QUARTER FEET WITH HER HANDS UP, GINNY WON'T BE MODELING ANY TIME SOON, THAT'S FOR SURE!!
HEE HEE HEE HEE HEE HEE HEE HEE HEE HEE HEE HEE HEE HEE HEE HEE HEE HEE

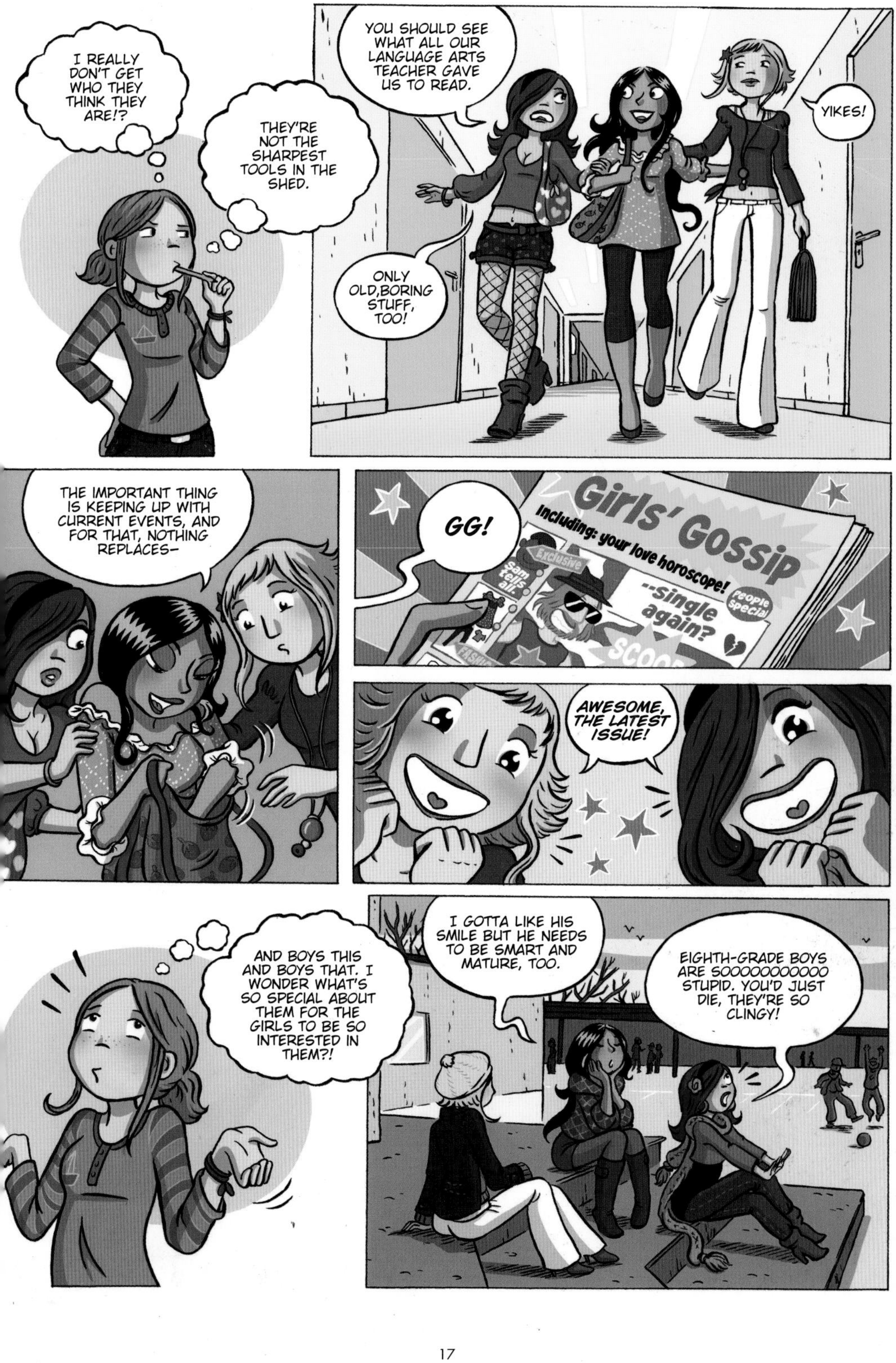
I REALLY DON'T GET WHO THEY THINK THEY ARE!?
THEY'RE NOT THE SHARPEST TOOLS IN THE SHED.
YOU SHOULD SEE WHAT ALL OUR LANGUAGE ARTS TEACHER GAVE US TO READ.
ONLY OLD,BORING STUFF, TOO!
YIKES!
THE IMPORTANT THING IS KEEPING UP WITH CURRENT EVENTS, AND FOR THAT, NOTHING REPLACES–
GG!
Girls' Gossip
Including: your love horoscope!
Exclusive
Sam tells all.
--single again?
People special
AWESOME, THE LATEST ISSUE!
AND BOYS THIS AND BOYS THAT. I WONDER WHAT'S SO SPECIAL ABOUT THEM FOR THE GIRLS TO BE SO INTERESTED IN THEM?!
I GOTTA LIKE HIS SMILE BUT HE NEEDS TO BE SMART AND MATURE, TOO.
EIGHTH-GRADE BOYS ARE SOOOOOOOOOOO STUPID. YOU'D JUST DIE, THEY'RE SO CLINGY!

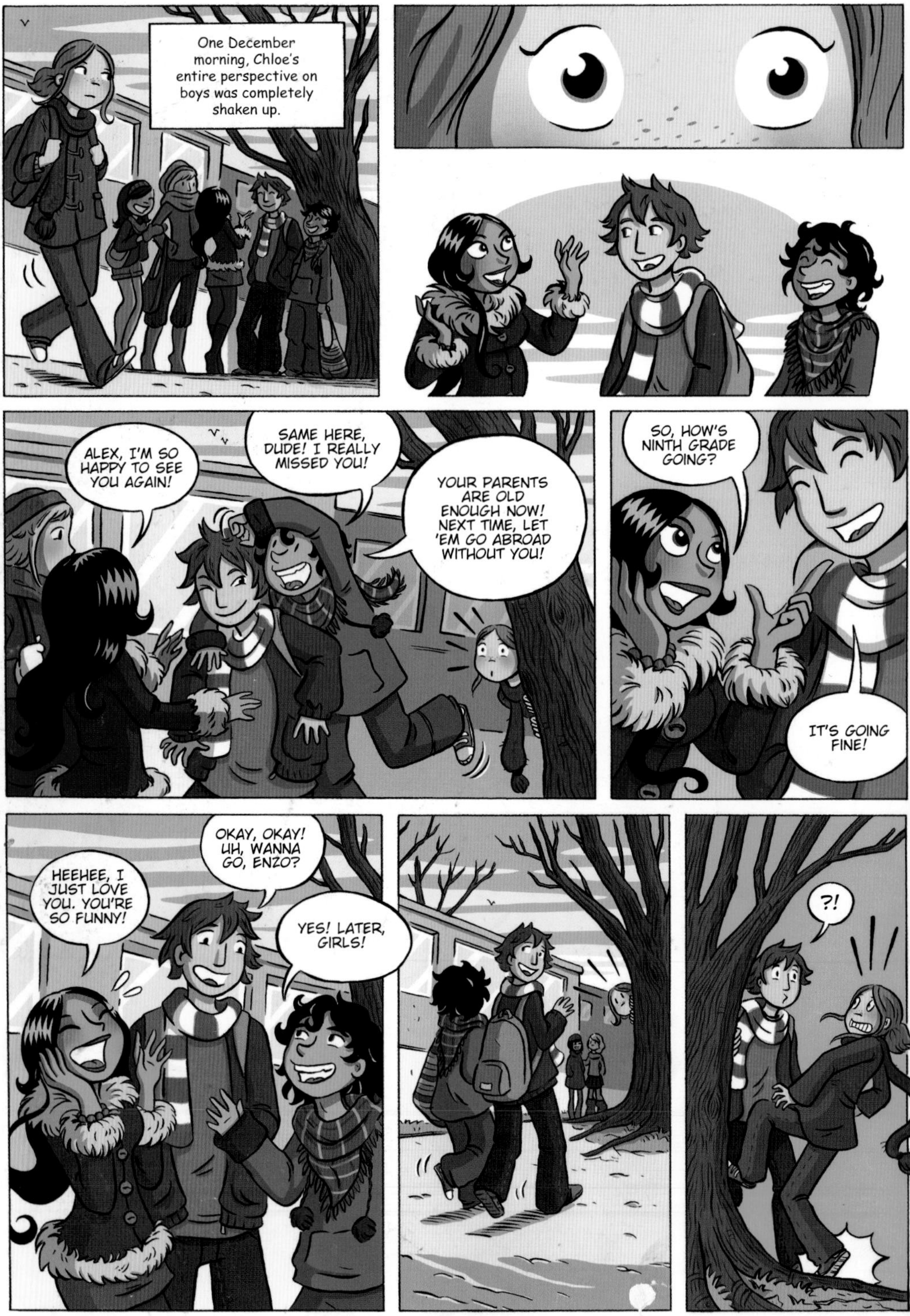
One December morning, Chloe's entire perspective on boys was completely shaken up.
ALEX, I'M SO HAPPY TO SEE YOU AGAIN!
SAME HERE, DUDE! I REALLY MISSED YOU!
YOUR PARENTS ARE OLD ENOUGH NOW! NEXT TIME, LET 'EM GO ABROAD WITHOUT YOU!
SO, HOW'S NINTH GRADE GOING?
IT'S GOING FINE!
HEEHEE, I JUST LOVE YOU. YOU'RE SO FUNNY!
OKAY, OKAY! UH, WANNA GO, ENZO?
YES! LATER, GIRLS!
?!

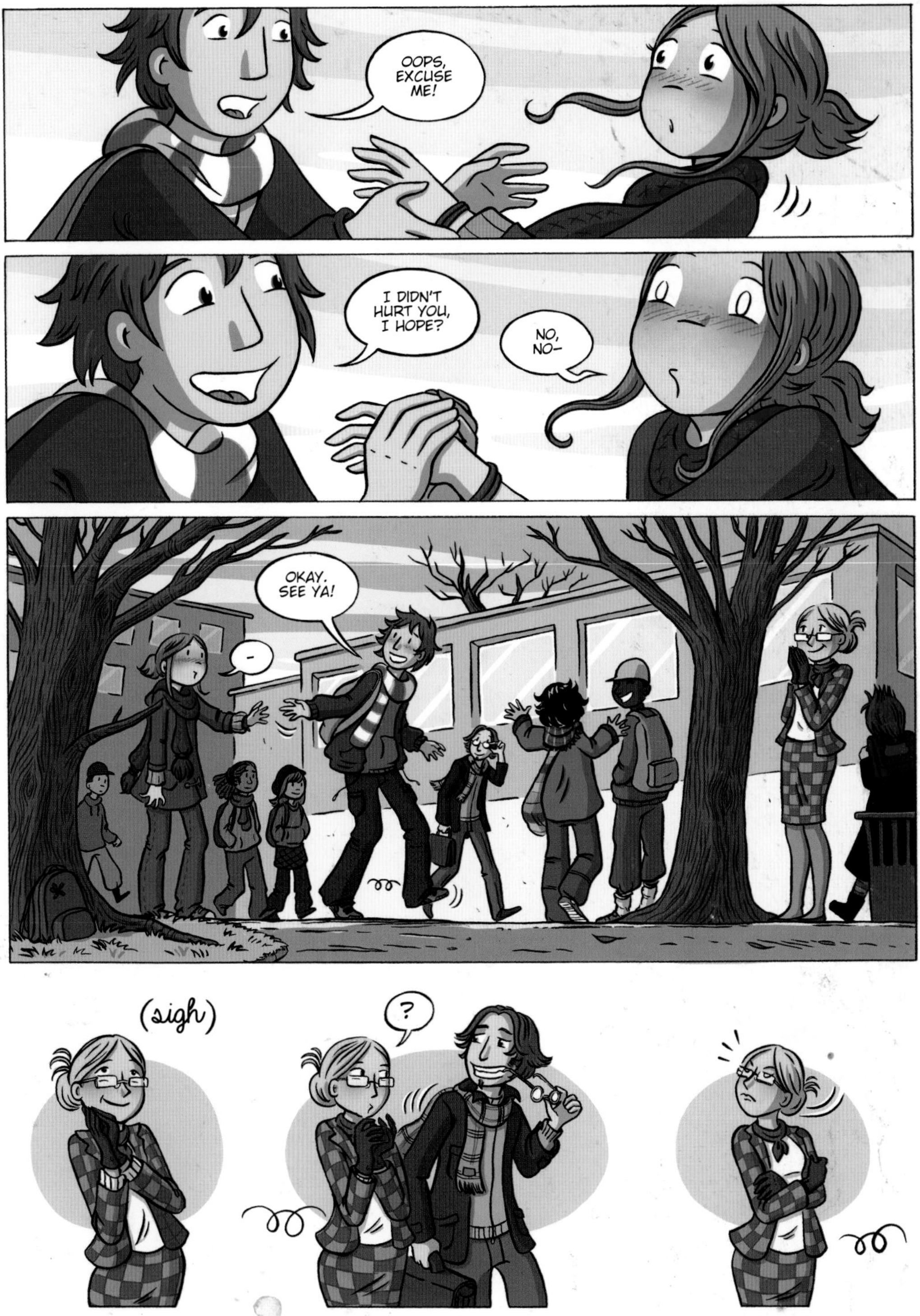
OOPS, EXCUSE ME!
I DIDN'T HURT YOU, I HOPE?
NO, NO-
OKAY. SEE YA!
-
(sigh)
?

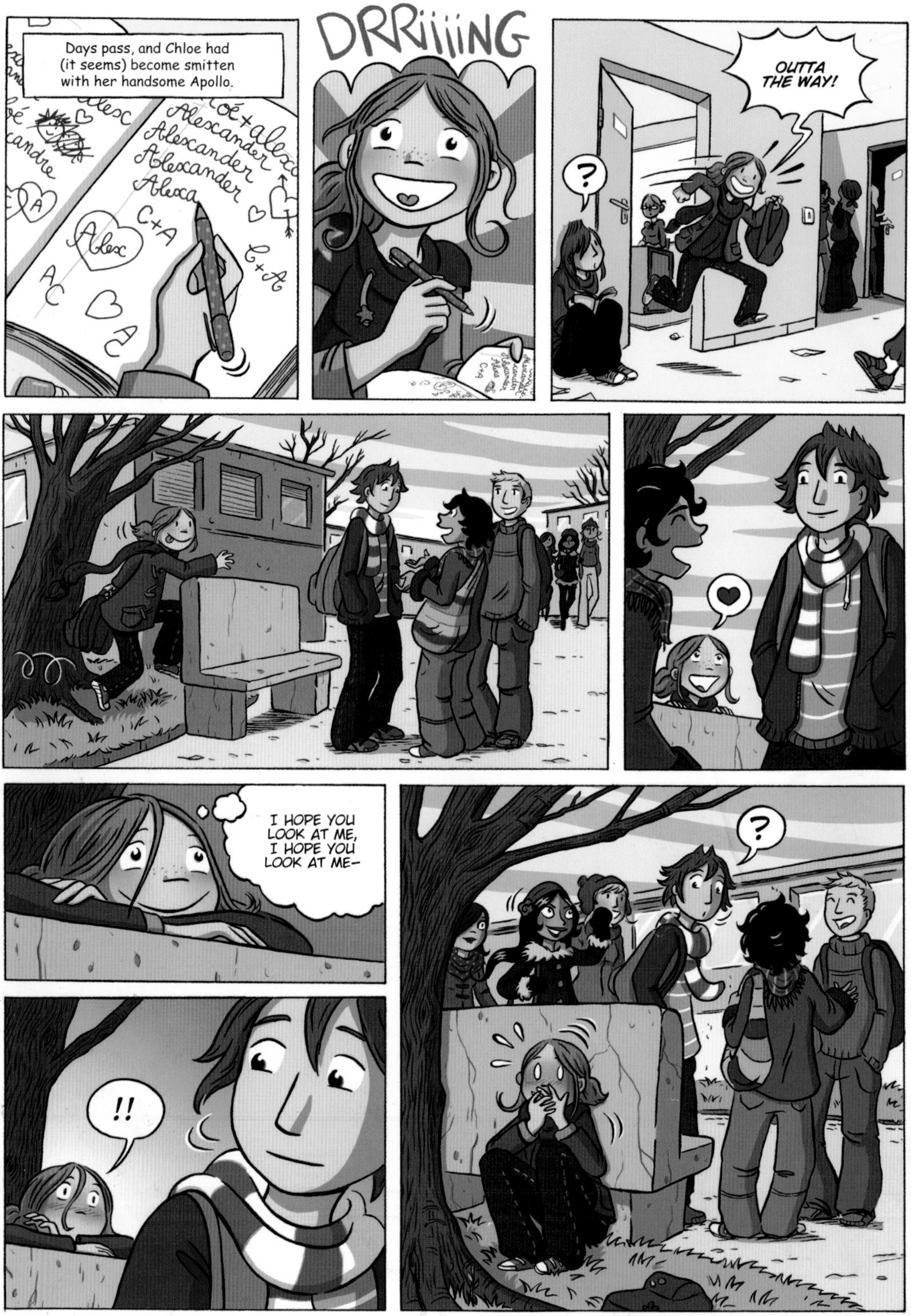
Days pass, and Chloe had (it seems) become smitten with her handsome Apollo.
Alexander
Alexander
Alexander
Alexa
Alex
C+A
C+A
DRRiiiiNG
?
OUTTA THE WAY!
I HOPE YOU LOOK AT ME, I HOPE YOU LOOK AT ME–
!!
?

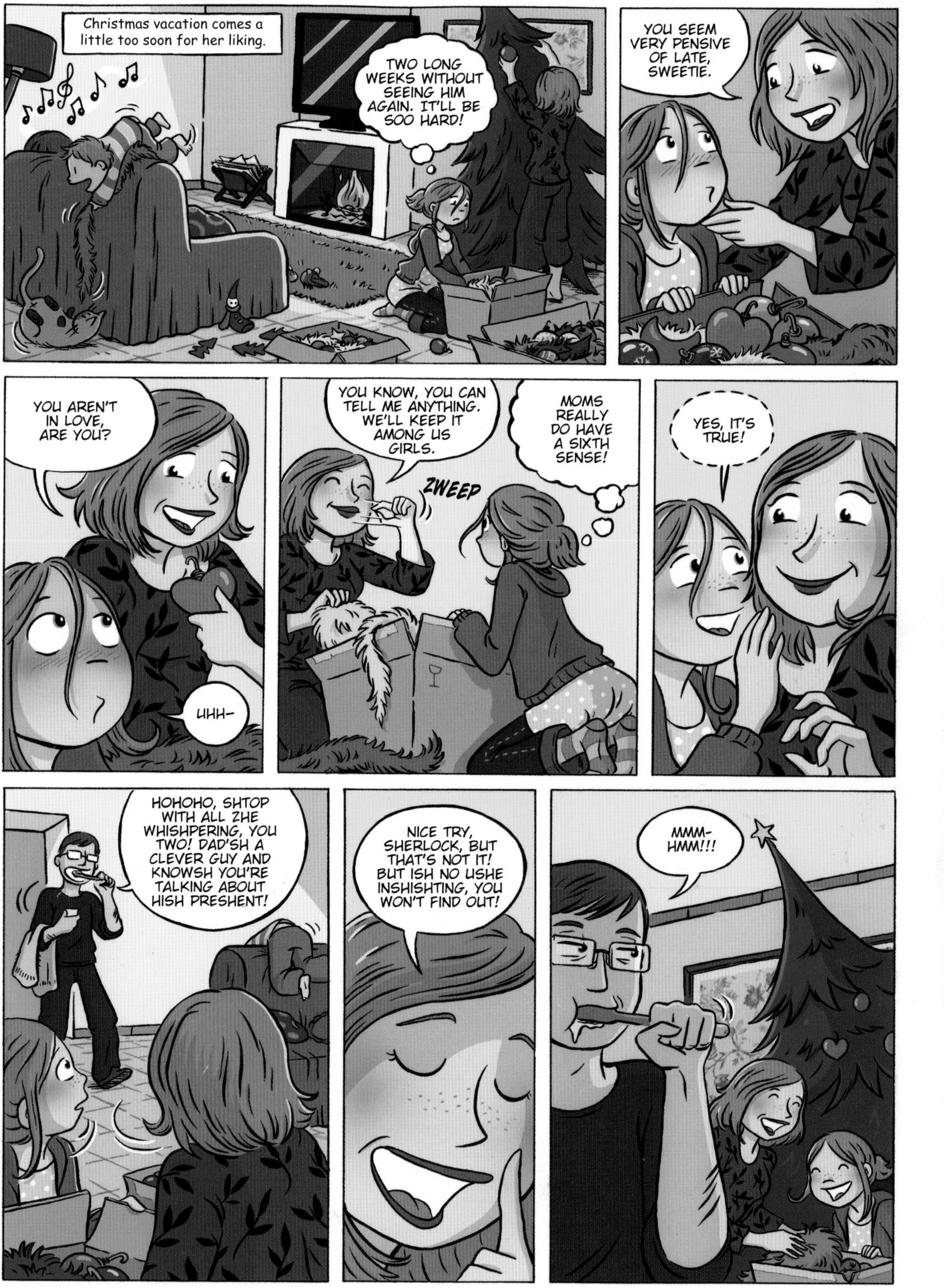
Christmas vacation comes a little too soon for her liking.
TWO LONG WEEKS WITHOUT SEEING HIM AGAIN. IT'LL BE SOO HARD!
YOU SEEM VERY PENSIVE OF LATE, SWEETIE.
YOU AREN'T IN LOVE, ARE YOU?
UHH-
YOU KNOW, YOU CAN TELL ME ANYTHING. WE'LL KEEP IT AMONG US GIRLS.
ZWEEP
MOMS REALLY DO HAVE A SIXTH SENSE!
YES, IT'S TRUE!
HOHOHO, SHTOP WITH ALL ZHE WHISHPERING, YOU TWO! DAD'SH A CLEVER GUY AND KNOWSH YOU'RE TALKING ABOUT HISH PRESHENT!
NICE TRY, SHERLOCK, BUT THAT'S NOT IT! BUT ISH NO USHE INSHISHTING, YOU WON'T FIND OUT!
MMM-HMM!!!

Report Card
1st Quarter

BLIN, Chloe or "Misty"
- Eighth Grade, Group C -

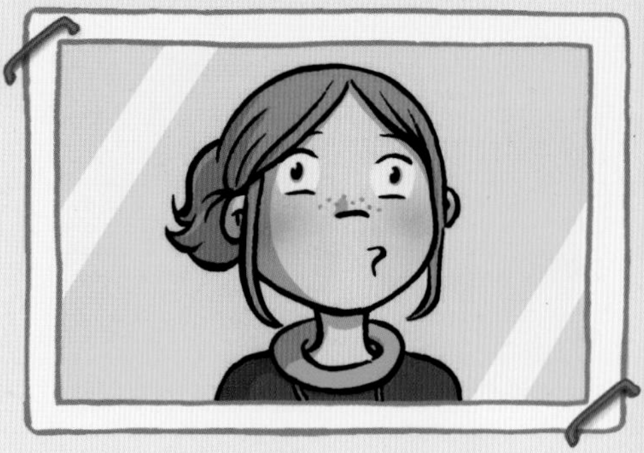

Subjects	Student Grade Averages	Suggestions for Improvement
Appearance	B	Average. A little originality would be welcome.
Self-confidence	D	Disastrous beginning. Annoying tendency to become withdrawn. You must forge ahead!
Observation Skills	A	Off to a very good start, but be careful about your inattentiveness.
Attractiveness	C-	Below average. Observing is fine, but the desire to be attractive mustn't be overlooked for all that.
Popularity	D	Mediocre. You build your own popularity!
Average for This Period	C	

General Comments:
Showed effort, certainly, but often Chloe lacks initiative. She often adopts a wait-and-see stance and lacks selfconfidence. The majority of readers advise her, from now on, to target her research. She will have to redouble her efforts in the 2nd Quarter.

Notification: this grade report is the original copy and must be preserved,

Signature of the home room teacher:

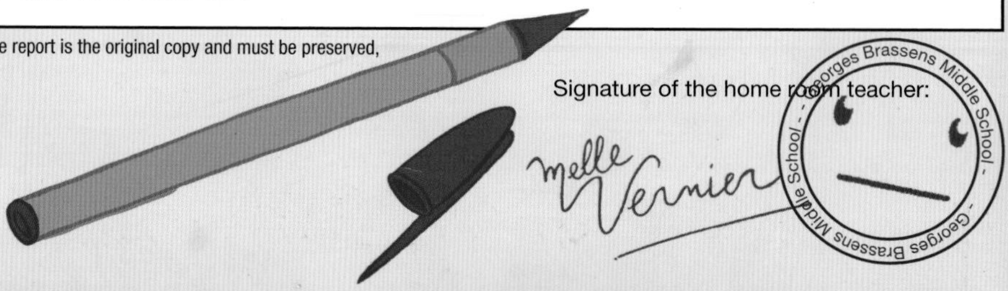
- Georges Brassens Middle School -
Melle Vernier

2nd Quarter

"Infiltration mode" engaged

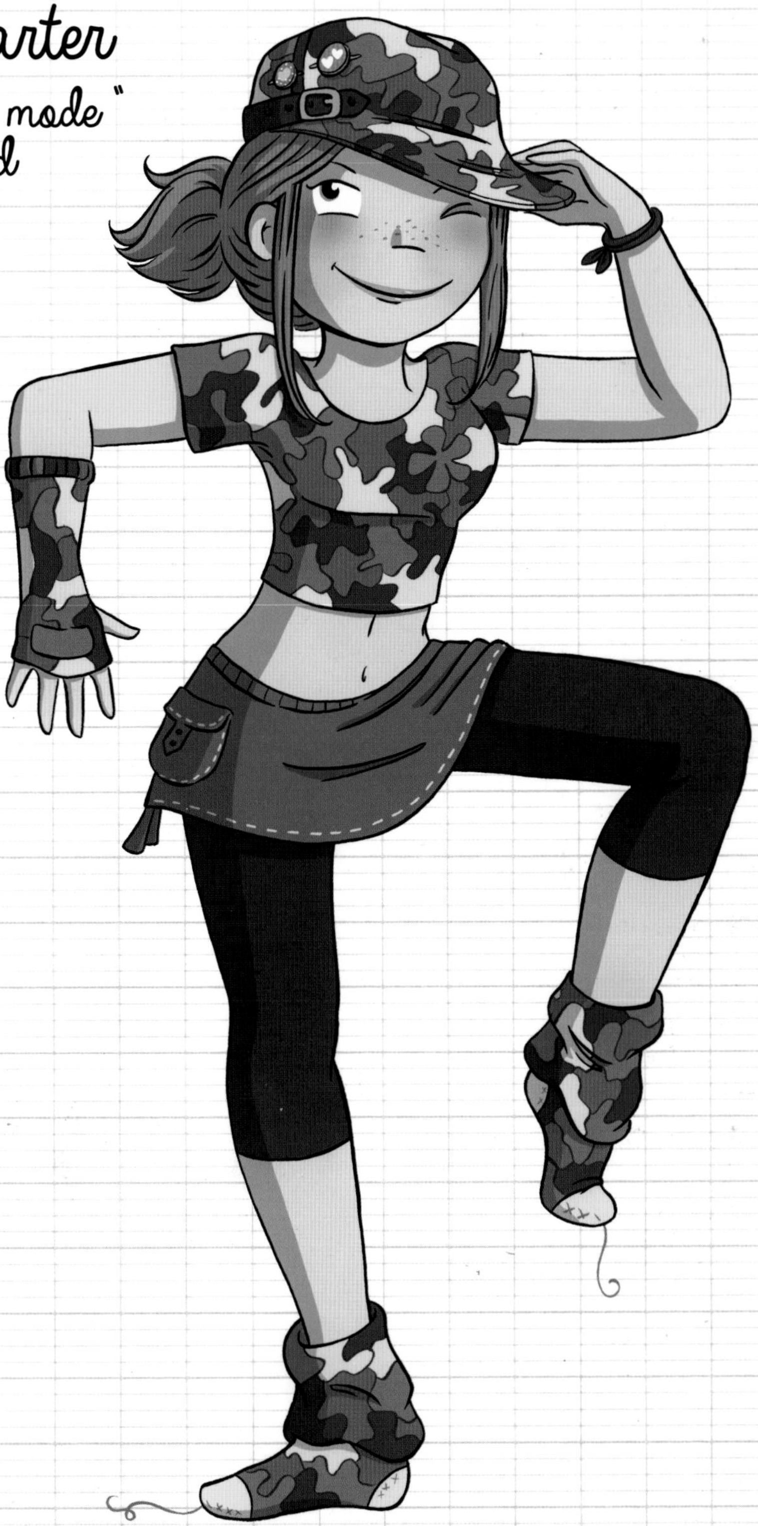

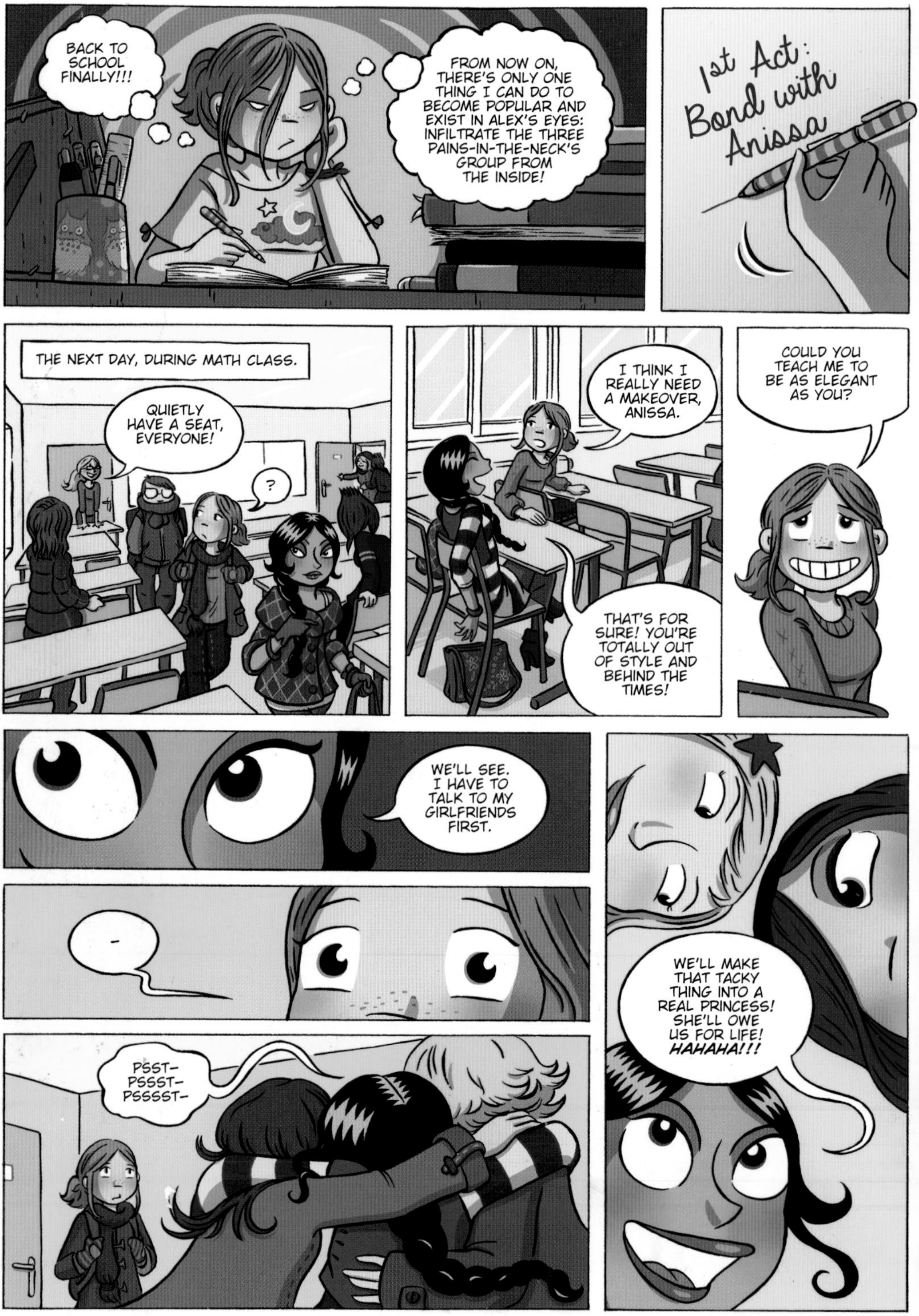
BACK TO SCHOOL FINALLY!!!
FROM NOW ON, THERE'S ONLY ONE THING I CAN DO TO BECOME POPULAR AND EXIST IN ALEX'S EYES: INFILTRATE THE THREE PAINS-IN-THE-NECK'S GROUP FROM THE INSIDE!
1st Act: Bond with Anissa
THE NEXT DAY, DURING MATH CLASS.
QUIETLY HAVE A SEAT, EVERYONE!
?
I THINK I REALLY NEED A MAKEOVER, ANISSA.
THAT'S FOR SURE! YOU'RE TOTALLY OUT OF STYLE AND BEHIND THE TIMES!
COULD YOU TEACH ME TO BE AS ELEGANT AS YOU?
WE'LL SEE. I HAVE TO TALK TO MY GIRLFRIENDS FIRST.
-
PSST- PSSST- PSSSST-
WE'LL MAKE THAT TACKY THING INTO A REAL PRINCESS! SHE'LL OWE US FOR LIFE! HAHAHA!!!

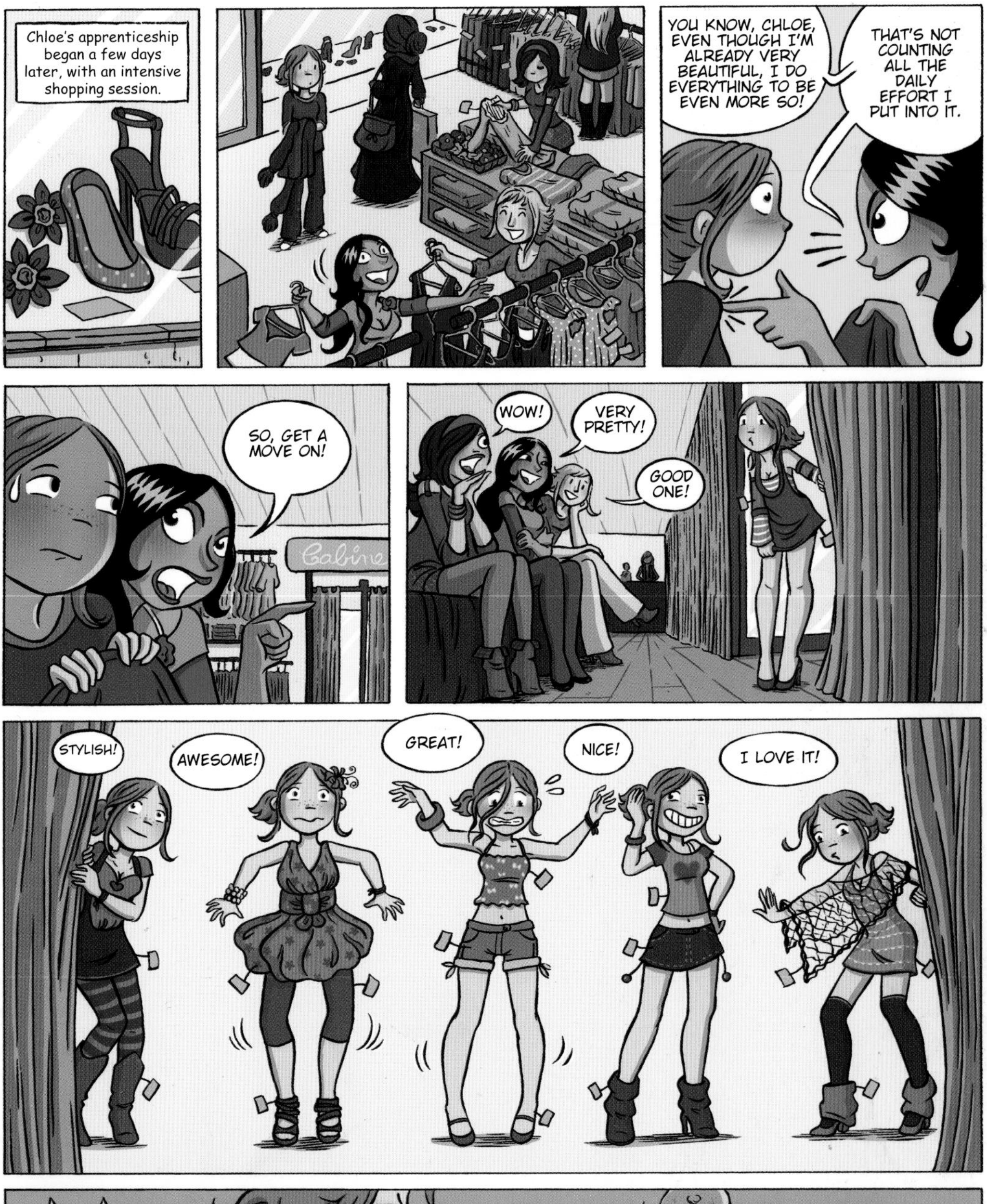
Chloe's apprenticeship began a few days later, with an intensive shopping session.
YOU KNOW, CHLOE, EVEN THOUGH I'M ALREADY VERY BEAUTIFUL, I DO EVERYTHING TO BE EVEN MORE SO!
THAT'S NOT COUNTING ALL THE DAILY EFFORT I PUT INTO IT.
SO, GET A MOVE ON!
Cabine
WOW!
VERY PRETTY!
GOOD ONE!
STYLISH!
AWESOME!
GREAT!
NICE!
I LOVE IT!
OW, OW, OW, STIFFNESS ALERT! MANDATORY STRETCHING TONIGHT!

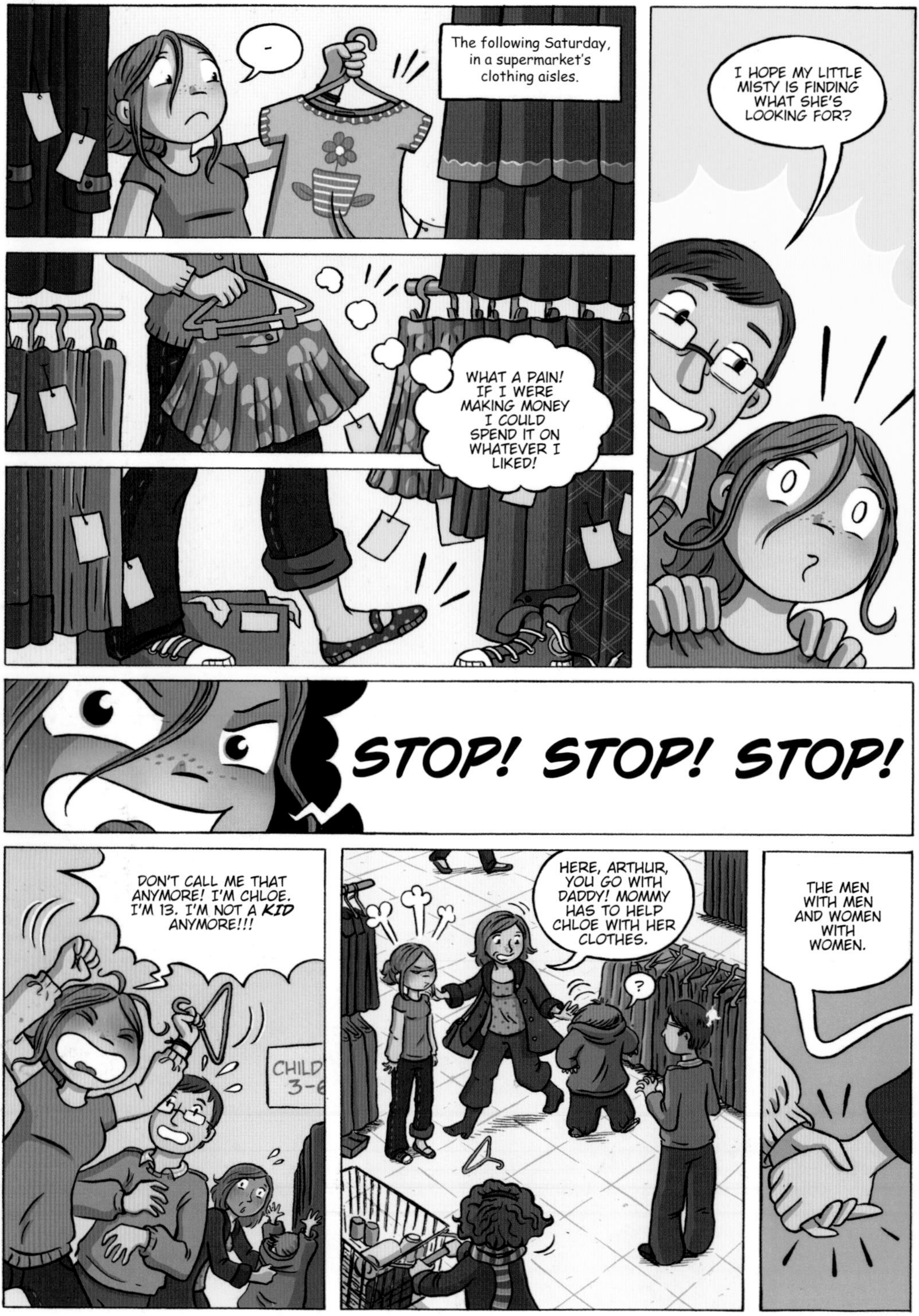
The following Saturday, in a supermarket's clothing aisles.
-
WHAT A PAIN! IF I WERE MAKING MONEY I COULD SPEND IT ON WHATEVER I LIKED!
I HOPE MY LITTLE MISTY IS FINDING WHAT SHE'S LOOKING FOR?
STOP! STOP! STOP!
DON'T CALL ME THAT ANYMORE! I'M CHLOE. I'M 13. I'M NOT A KID ANYMORE!!!
HERE, ARTHUR, YOU GO WITH DADDY! MOMMY HAS TO HELP CHLOE WITH HER CLOTHES.
?
THE MEN WITH MEN AND WOMEN WITH WOMEN.

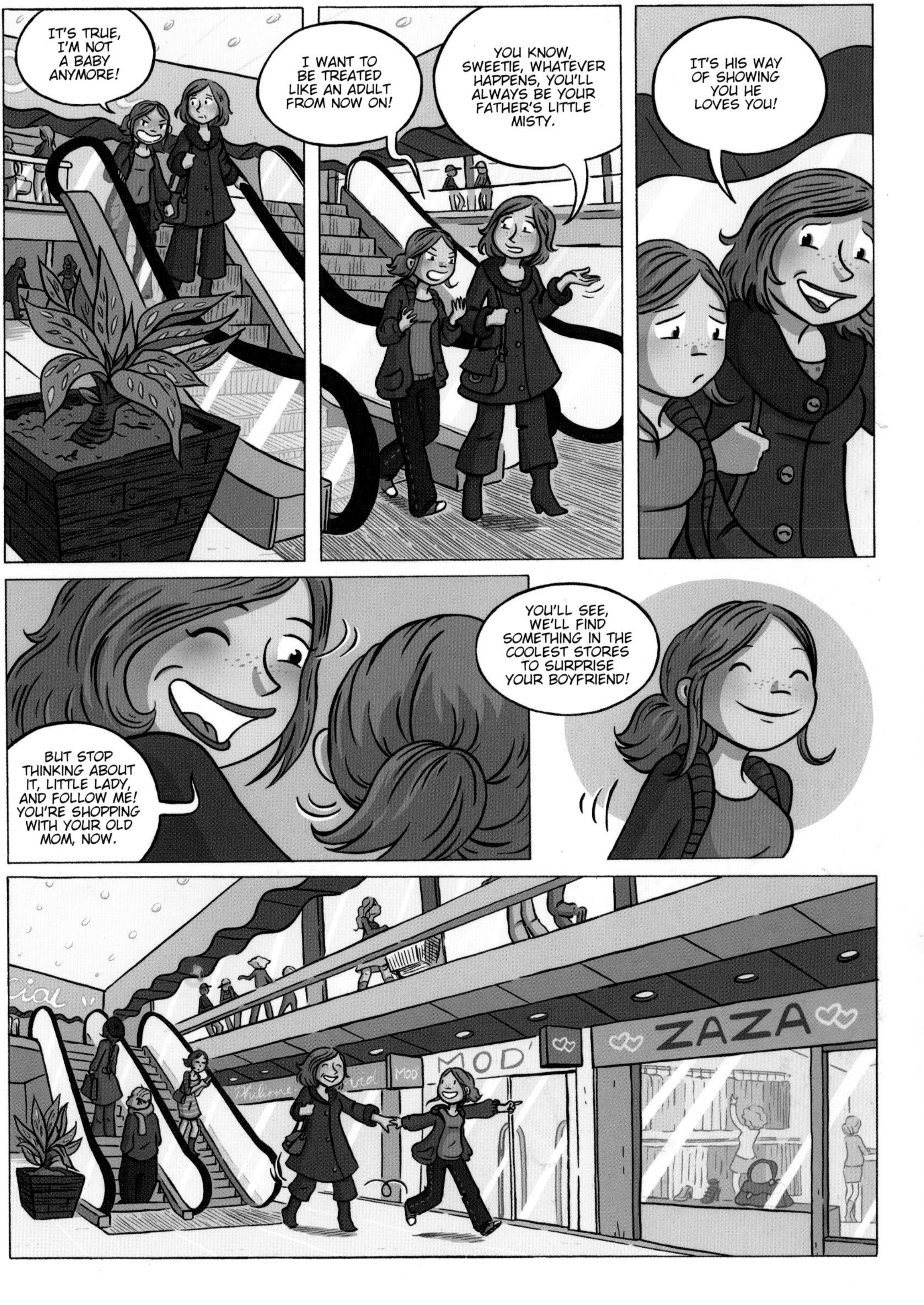
IT'S TRUE, I'M NOT A BABY ANYMORE!
I WANT TO BE TREATED LIKE AN ADULT FROM NOW ON!
YOU KNOW, SWEETIE, WHATEVER HAPPENS, YOU'LL ALWAYS BE YOUR FATHER'S LITTLE MISTY.
IT'S HIS WAY OF SHOWING YOU HE LOVES YOU!
BUT STOP THINKING ABOUT IT, LITTLE LADY, AND FOLLOW ME! YOU'RE SHOPPING WITH YOUR OLD MOM, NOW.
YOU'LL SEE, WE'LL FIND SOMETHING IN THE COOLEST STORES TO SURPRISE YOUR BOYFRIEND!
MOD'
ZAZA

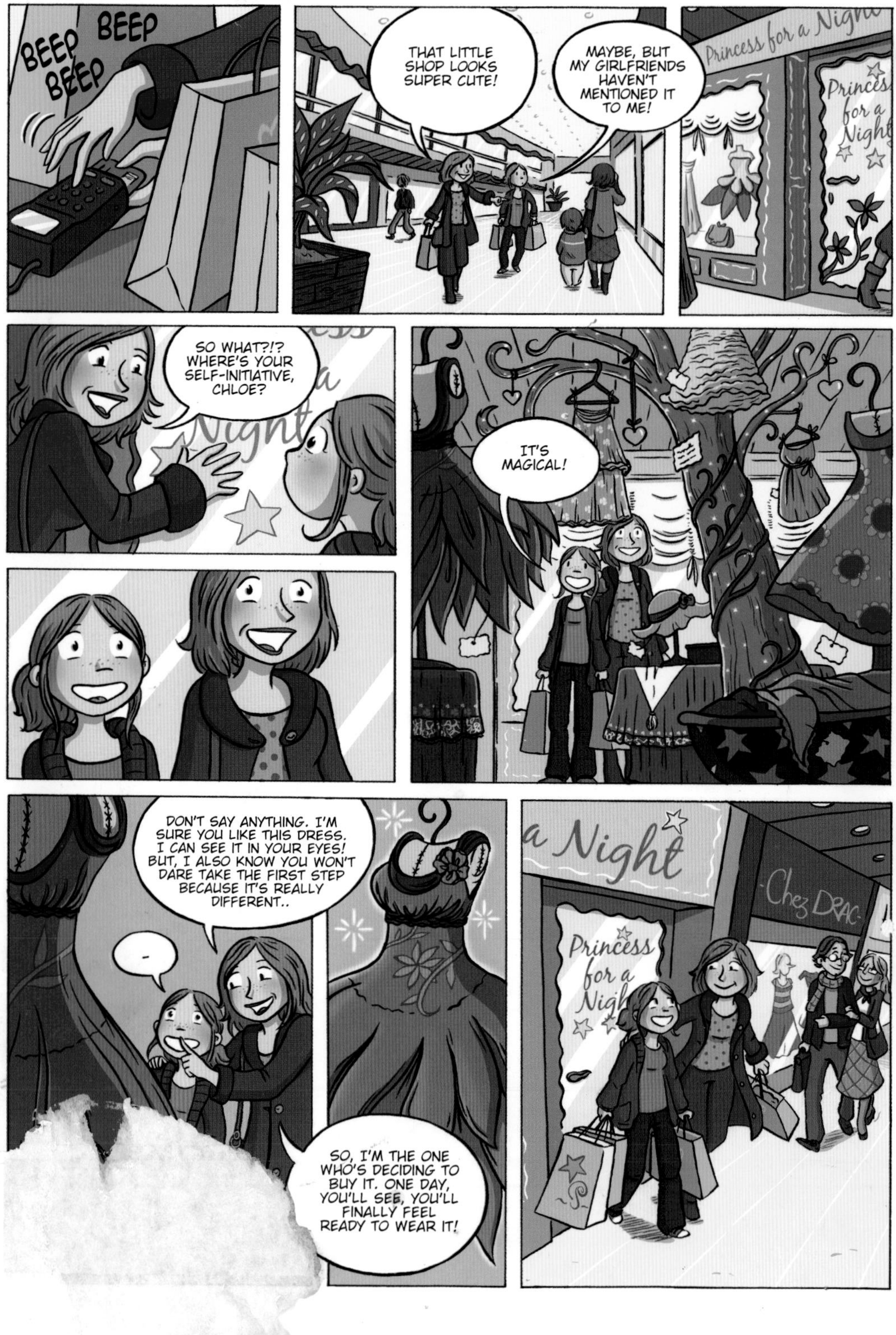
BEEP
BEEP
BEEP
THAT LITTLE SHOP LOOKS SUPER CUTE!
MAYBE, BUT MY GIRLFRIENDS HAVEN'T MENTIONED IT TO ME!
Princess for a Night
Princess for a Night
SO WHAT?!? WHERE'S YOUR SELF-INITIATIVE, CHLOE?
IT'S MAGICAL!
DON'T SAY ANYTHING. I'M SURE YOU LIKE THIS DRESS. I CAN SEE IT IN YOUR EYES! BUT, I ALSO KNOW YOU WON'T DARE TAKE THE FIRST STEP BECAUSE IT'S REALLY DIFFERENT..
-
SO, I'M THE ONE WHO'S DECIDING TO BUY IT. ONE DAY, YOU'LL SEE, YOU'LL FINALLY FEEL READY TO WEAR IT!
a Night
Chez DRAC
Princess for a Nigh

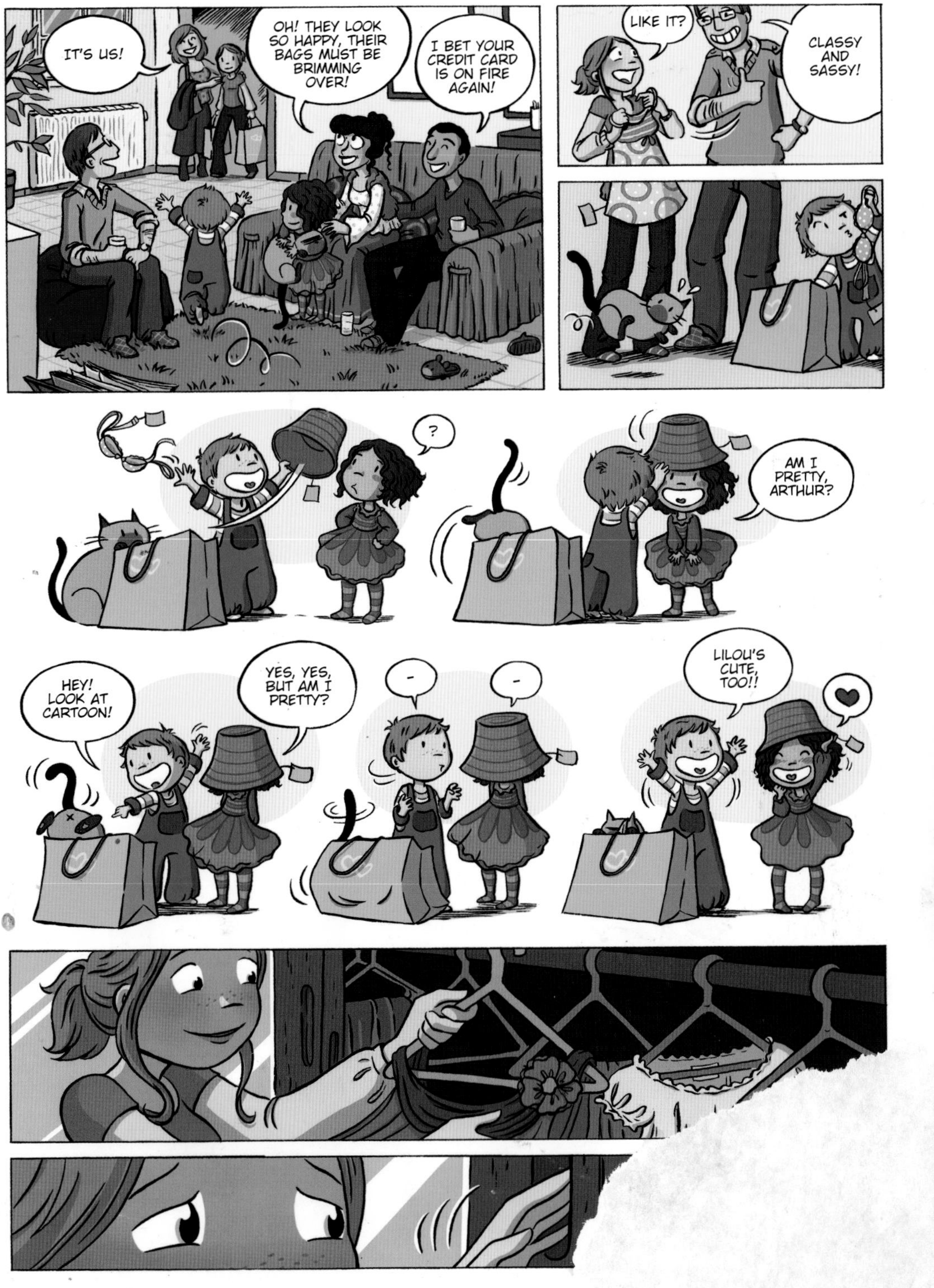
IT'S US!
OH! THEY LOOK SO HAPPY, THEIR BAGS MUST BE BRIMMING OVER!
I BET YOUR CREDIT CARD IS ON FIRE AGAIN!
LIKE IT?
CLASSY AND SASSY!
?
AM I PRETTY, ARTHUR?
HEY! LOOK AT CARTOON!
YES, YES, BUT AM I PRETTY?
-
-
LILOU'S CUTE, TOO!!

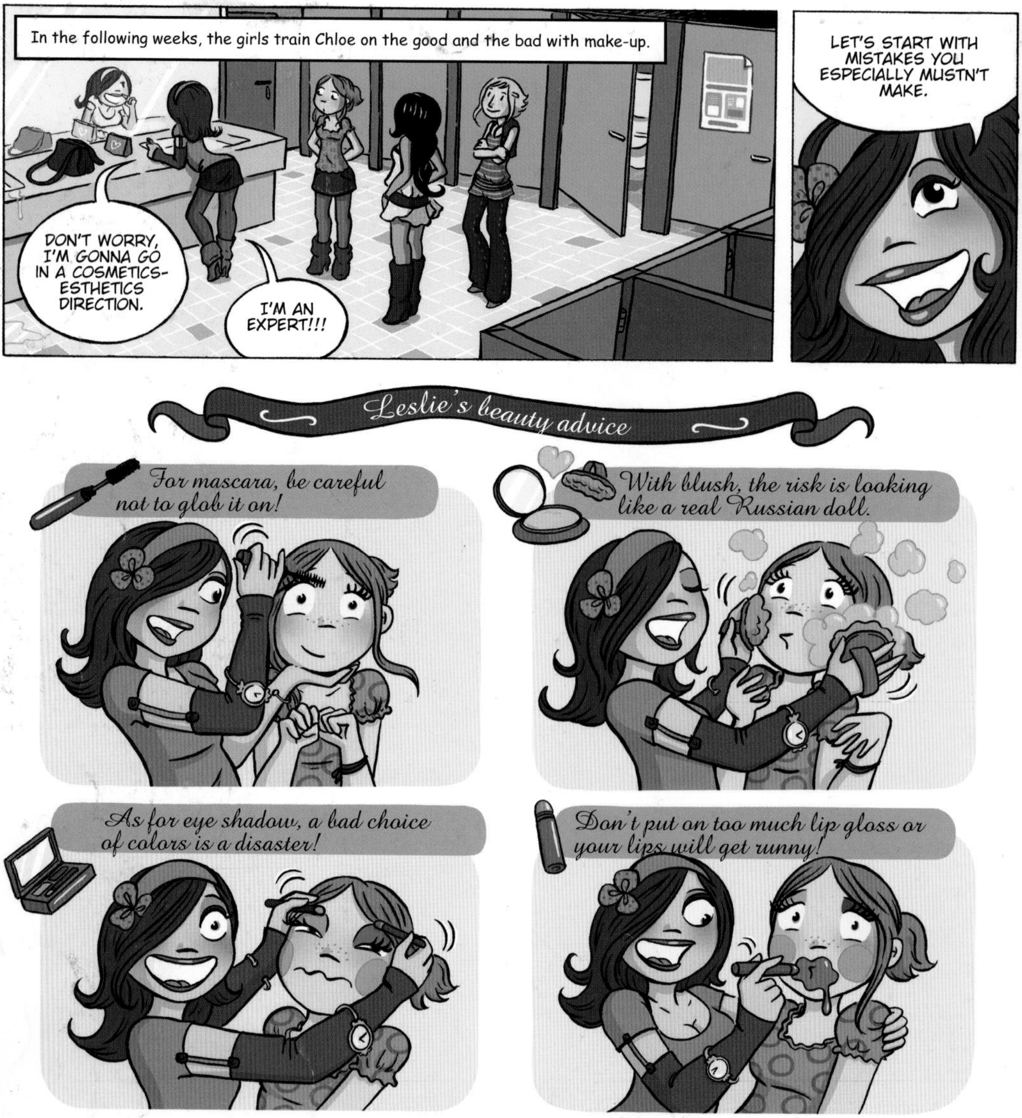

In the following weeks, the girls train Chloe on the good and the bad with make-up.
DON'T WORRY, I'M GONNA GO IN A COSMETICS-ESTHETICS DIRECTION.
I'M AN EXPERT!!!
LET'S START WITH MISTAKES YOU ESPECIALLY MUSTN'T MAKE.
Leslie's beauty advice
For mascara, be careful not to glob it on!
With blush, the risk is looking like a real Russian doll.
As for eye shadow, a bad choice of colors is a disaster!
Don't put on too much lip gloss or your lips will get runny!
OOOOWWW!
AND LET'S NOT FORGET, SOMETIMES YOU HAVE TO SUFFER TO BE BEAUTIFUL!

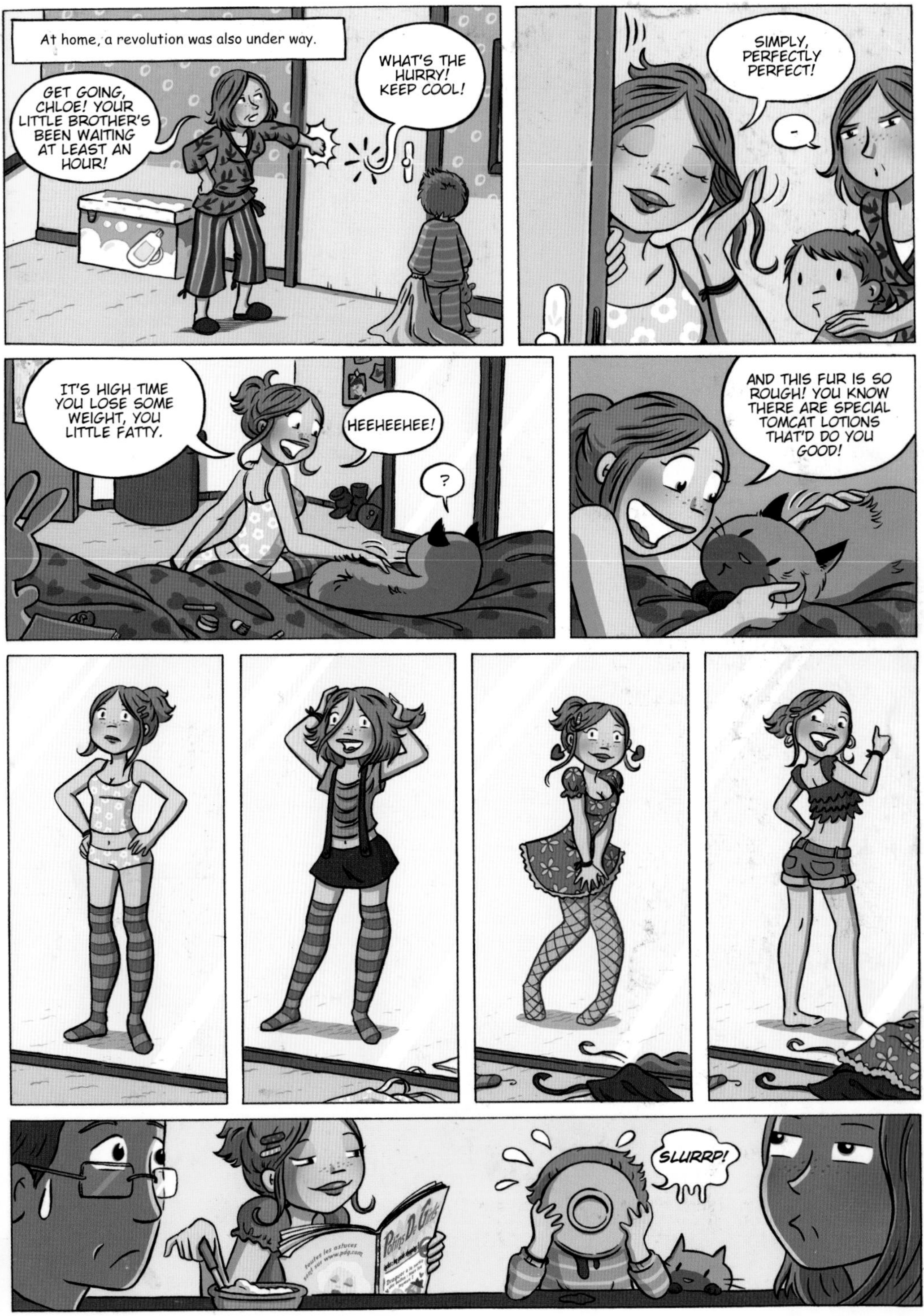
At home, a revolution was also under way.
GET GOING, CHLOE! YOUR LITTLE BROTHER'S BEEN WAITING AT LEAST AN HOUR!
WHAT'S THE HURRY! KEEP COOL!
SIMPLY, PERFECTLY PERFECT!
-
IT'S HIGH TIME YOU LOSE SOME WEIGHT, YOU LITTLE FATTY.
HEEHEEHEE!
?
AND THIS FUR IS SO ROUGH! YOU KNOW THERE ARE SPECIAL TOMCAT LOTIONS THAT'D DO YOU GOOD!
SLURRP!

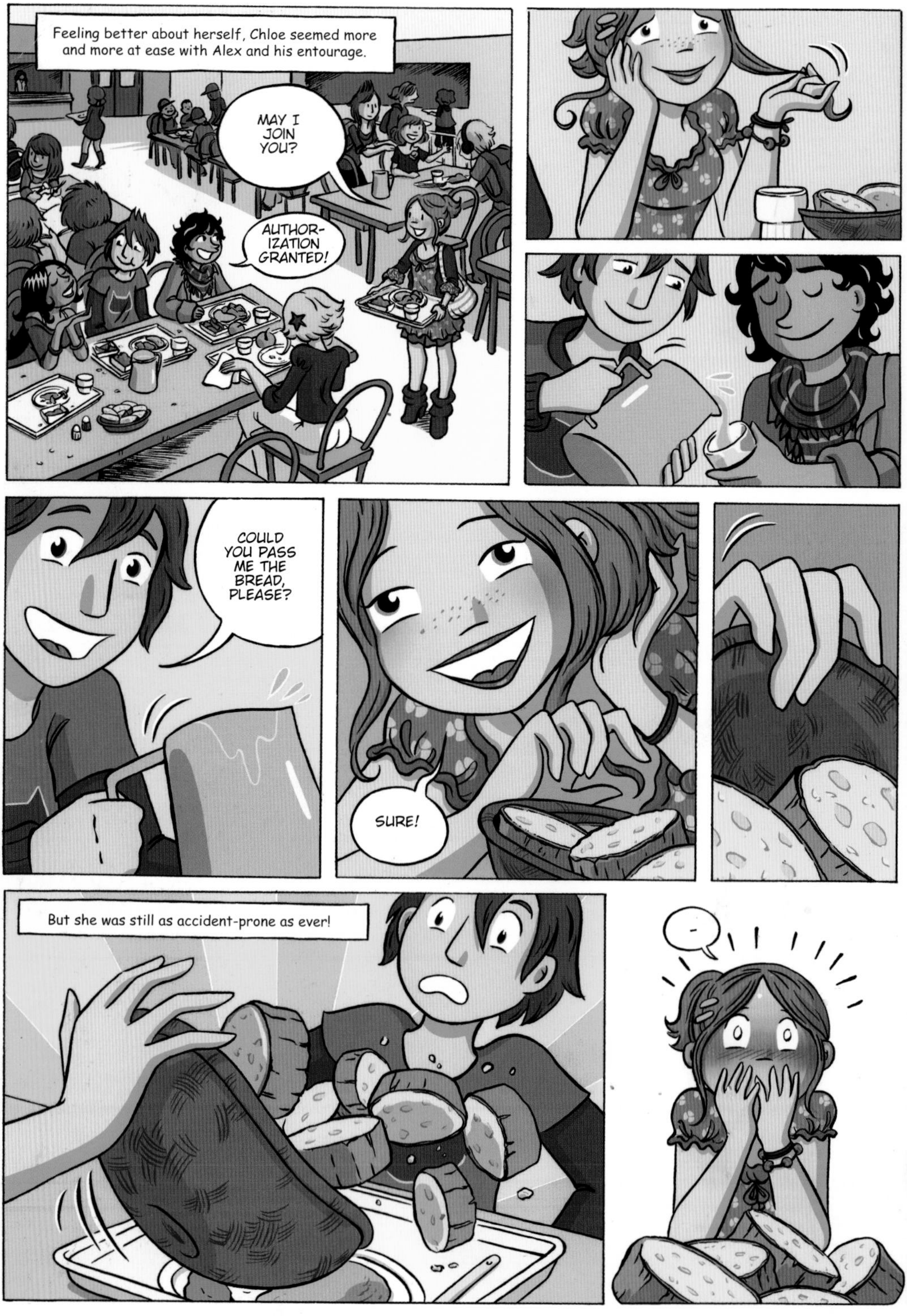

Feeling better about herself, Chloe seemed more and more at ease with Alex and his entourage.
MAY I JOIN YOU?
AUTHORIZATION GRANTED!
COULD YOU PASS ME THE BREAD, PLEASE?
SURE!
But she was still as accident-prone as ever!
-

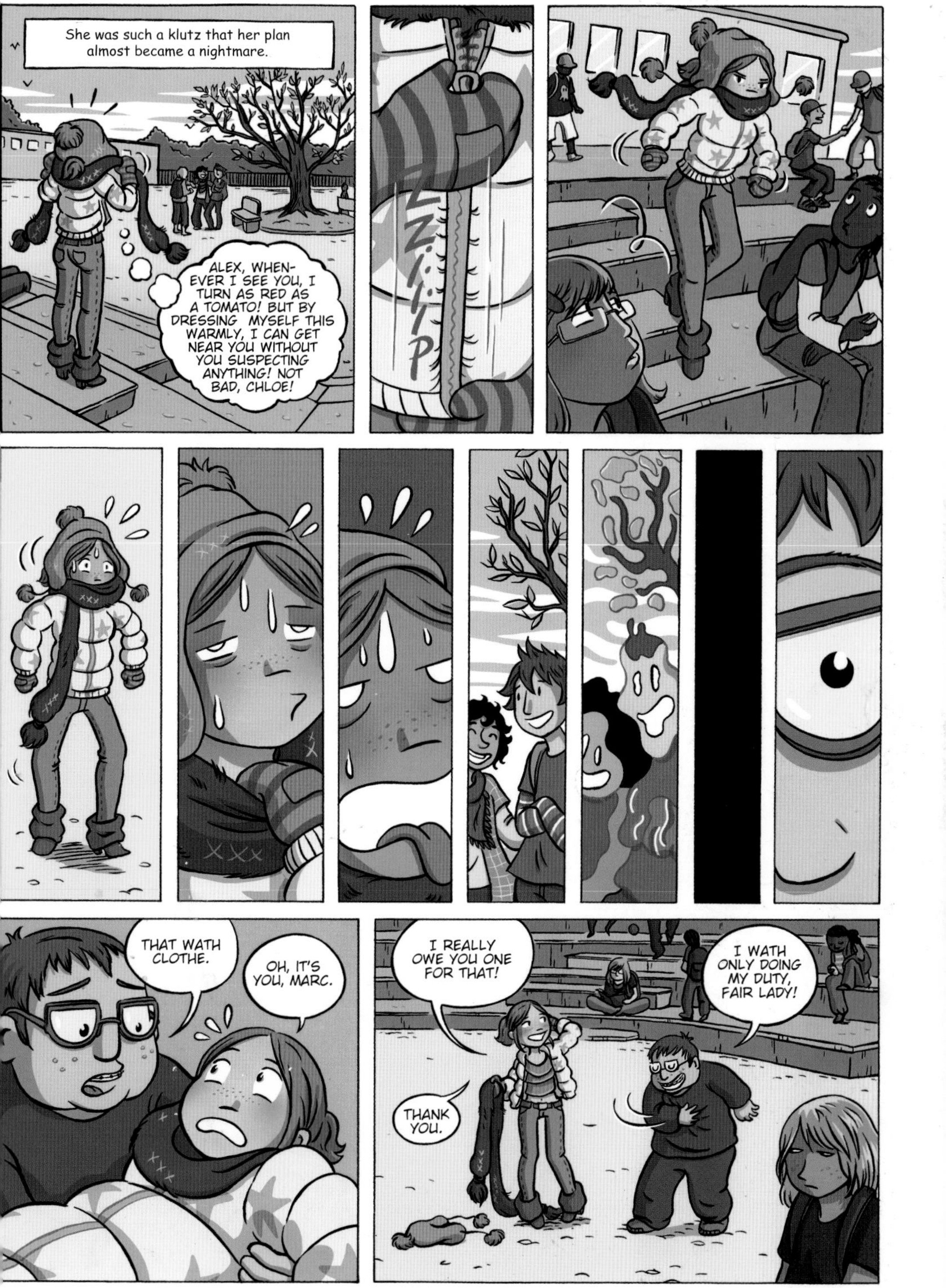
She was such a klutz that her plan almost became a nightmare.
ALEX, WHEN-EVER I SEE YOU, I TURN AS RED AS A TOMATO! BUT BY DRESSING MYSELF THIS WARMLY, I CAN GET NEAR YOU WITHOUT YOU SUSPECTING ANYTHING! NOT BAD, CHLOE!
ZZIIIP
THAT WATH CLOTHE.
OH, IT'S YOU, MARC.
I REALLY OWE YOU ONE FOR THAT!
THANK YOU.
I WATH ONLY DOING MY DUTY, FAIR LADY!

However, some nights she let herself take that single step from a nightmare to a dream.

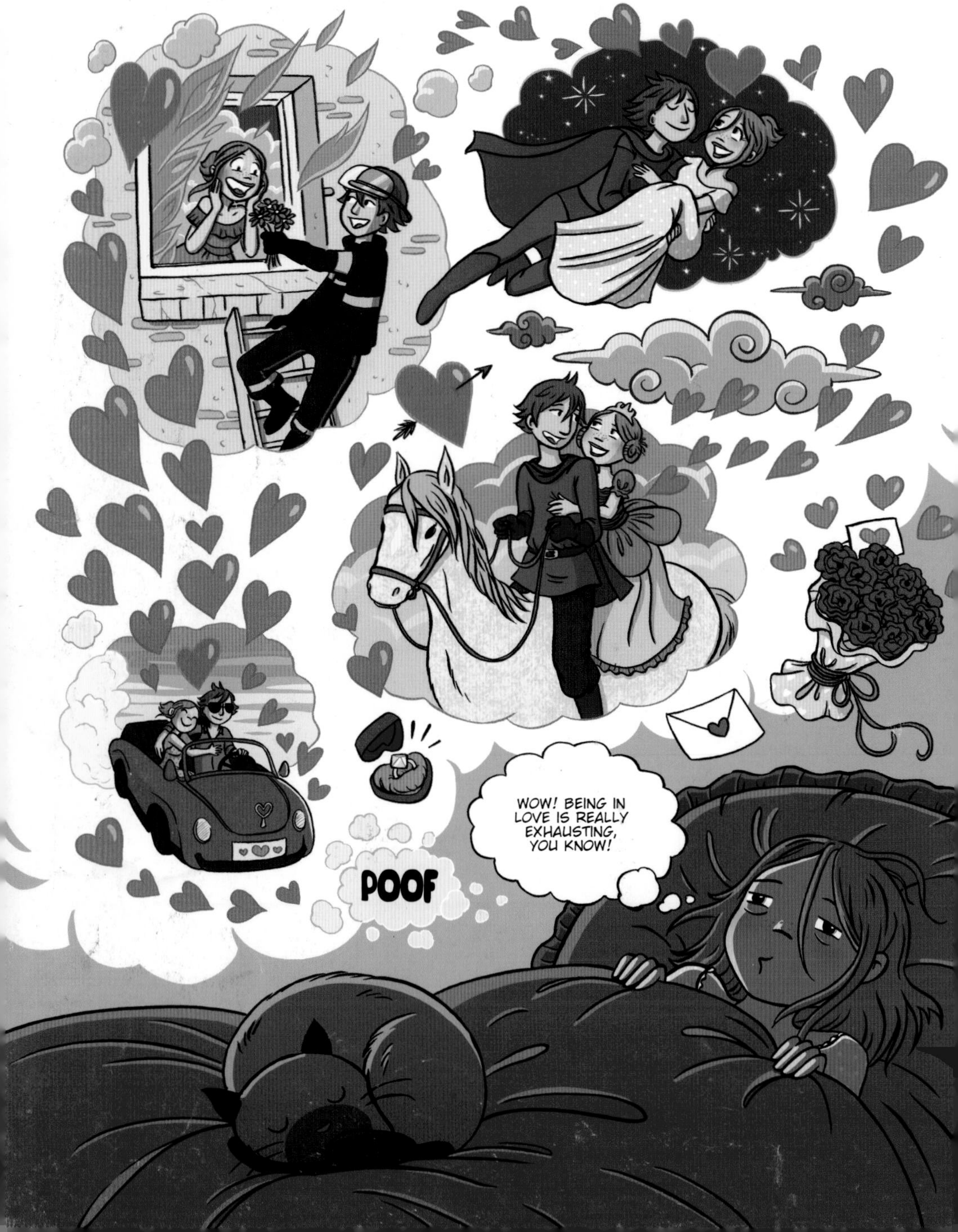
WOW! BEING IN LOVE IS REALLY EXHAUSTING, YOU KNOW!
POOF

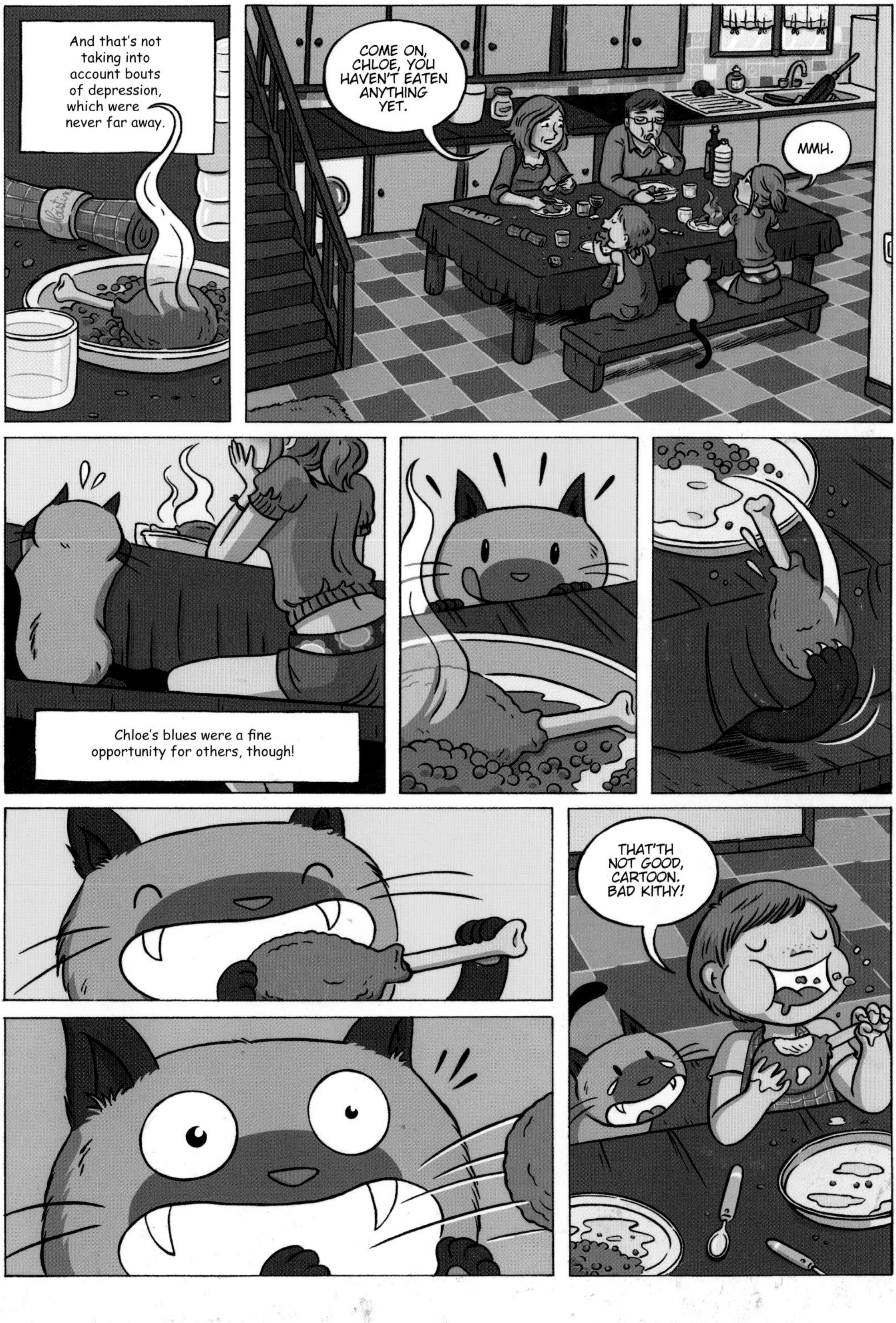
And that's not taking into account bouts of depression, which were never far away.
COME ON, CHLOE, YOU HAVEN'T EATEN ANYTHING YET.
MMH.
Chloe's blues were a fine opportunity for others, though!
THAT'TH NOT GOOD, CARTOON. BAD KITHY!

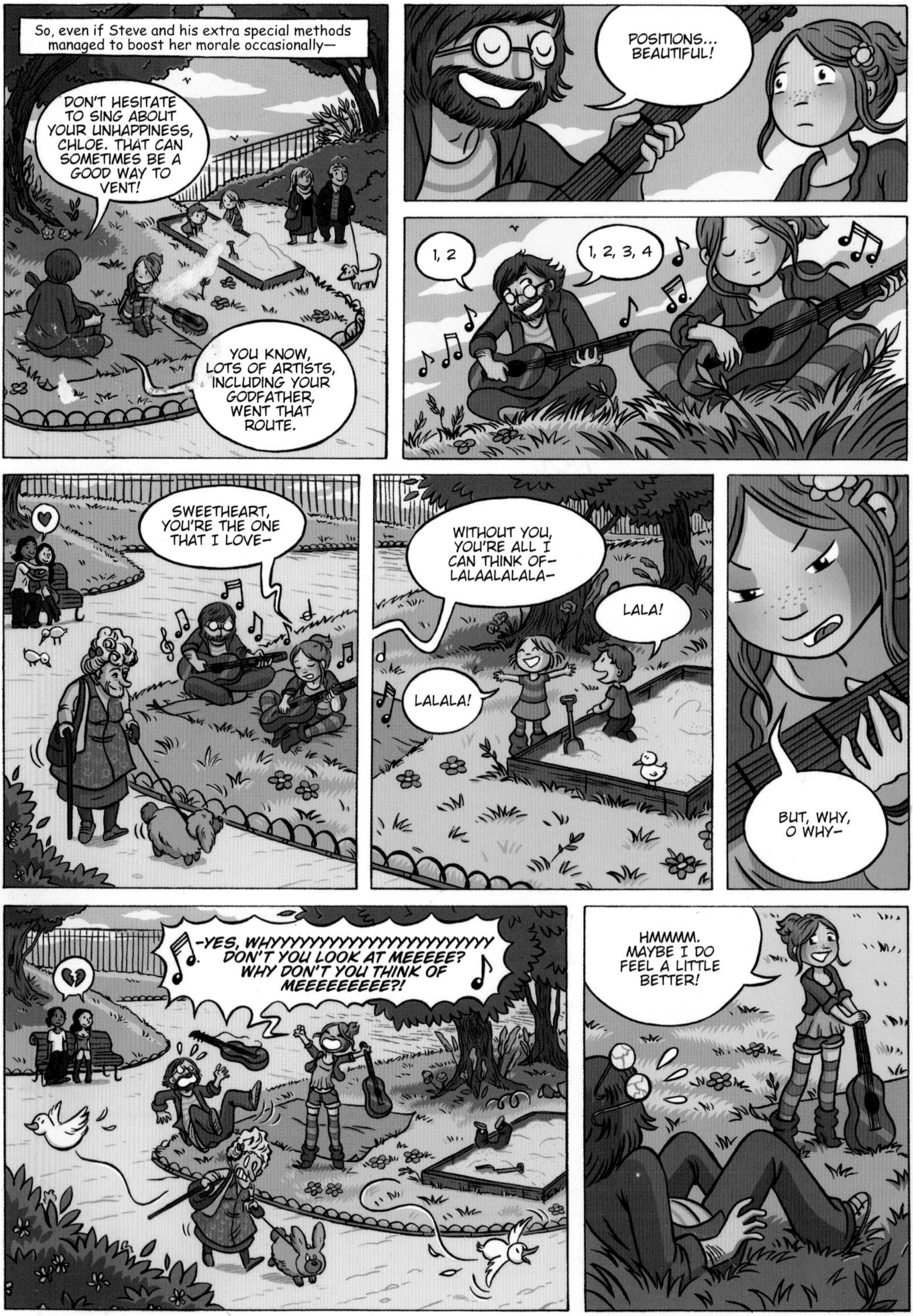
So, even if Steve and his extra special methods managed to boost her morale occasionally—
DON'T HESITATE TO SING ABOUT YOUR UNHAPPINESS, CHLOE. THAT CAN SOMETIMES BE A GOOD WAY TO VENT!
YOU KNOW, LOTS OF ARTISTS, INCLUDING YOUR GODFATHER, WENT THAT ROUTE.
POSITIONS... BEAUTIFUL!
1, 2
1, 2, 3, 4
SWEETHEART, YOU'RE THE ONE THAT I LOVE-
WITHOUT YOU, YOU'RE ALL I CAN THINK OF- LALAALALALA-
LALA!
LALALA!
BUT, WHY, O WHY-
-YES, WHYYYYYYYYYYYYYYYYYYYYYY DON'T YOU LOOK AT MEEEEE? WHY DON'T YOU THINK OF MEEEEEEEEE?!
HMMMM. MAYBE I DO FEEL A LITTLE BETTER!

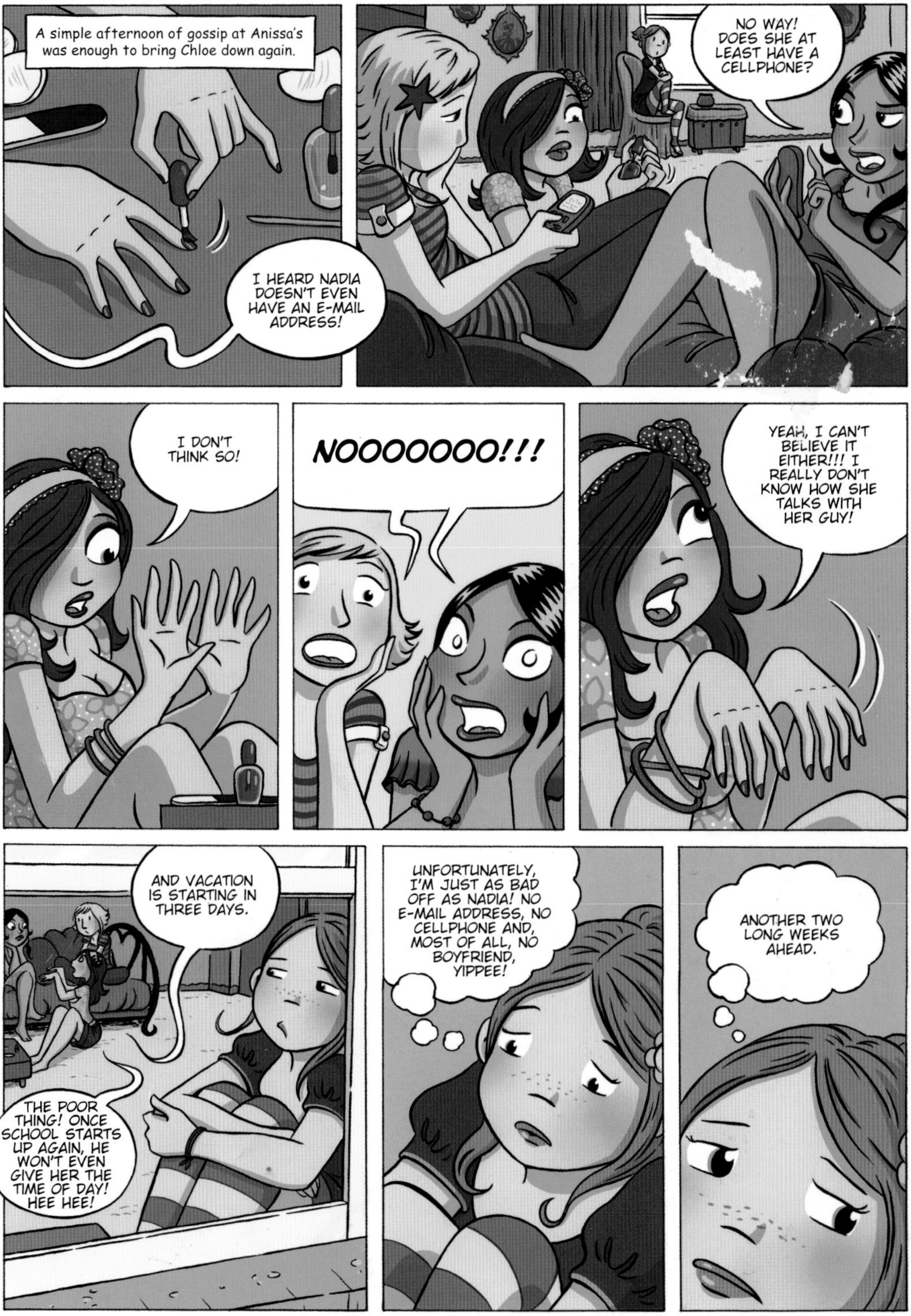
A simple afternoon of gossip at Anissa's was enough to bring Chloe down again.
I HEARD NADIA DOESN'T EVEN HAVE AN E-MAIL ADDRESS!
NO WAY! DOES SHE AT LEAST HAVE A CELLPHONE?
I DON'T THINK SO!
NOOOOOOO!!!
YEAH, I CAN'T BELIEVE IT EITHER!!! I REALLY DON'T KNOW HOW SHE TALKS WITH HER GUY!
AND VACATION IS STARTING IN THREE DAYS.
THE POOR THING! ONCE SCHOOL STARTS UP AGAIN, HE WON'T EVEN GIVE HER THE TIME OF DAY! HEE HEE!
UNFORTUNATELY, I'M JUST AS BAD OFF AS NADIA! NO E-MAIL ADDRESS, NO CELLPHONE AND, MOST OF ALL, NO BOYFRIEND, YIPPEE!
ANOTHER TWO LONG WEEKS AHEAD.

Report Card

2nd Quarter

BLIN, Chloe or "Misty"
- Eighth Grade, Group C -

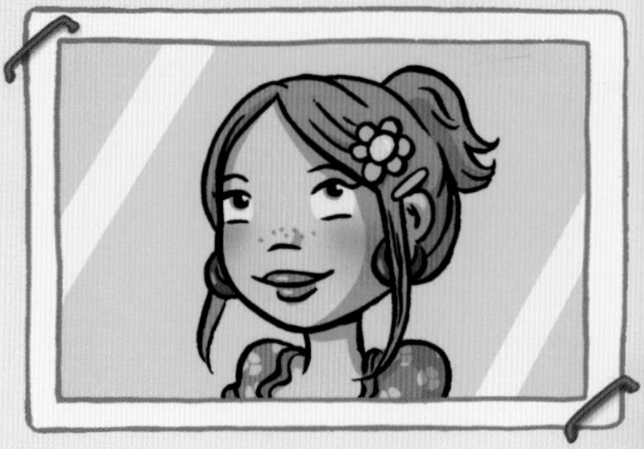

Subjects	Student Grade Averages	Suggestions for Improvement
Appearance	B	Truly invested. But be careful not to worry too much over it, or else you won't know which way to turn!
Self-confidence	C	Even with highs and lows in succession, good instances of taking the initiative are to be noted. Encouraging.
Observation Skills	A	Continued interest in the material. Good job.
Attractiveness	B	Doing better. Motivated to participate.
Popularity	C	Keep going, success is at the end of the road.
Average for This Period	B	

General Comments:
Chloe made notable progress this quarter. She's undeniably more comfortable with herself. Readers are aware of that and support her.

Notification: this grade report is the original copy and must be preserved,

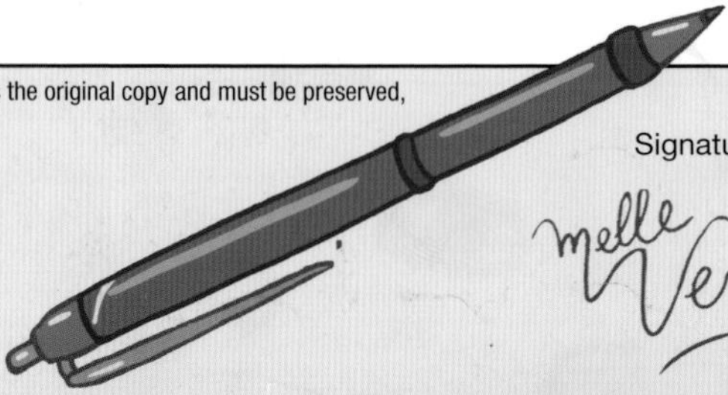

Signature of the home room teacher:

Melle Vernier

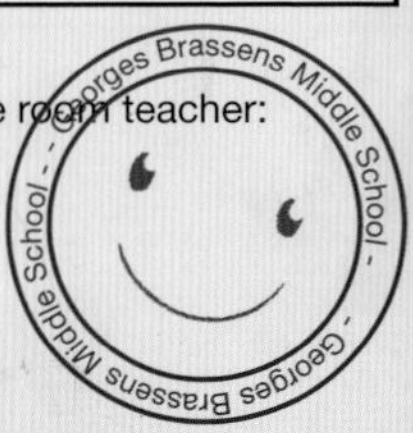
- Georges Brassens Middle School - Georges Brassens Middle School -

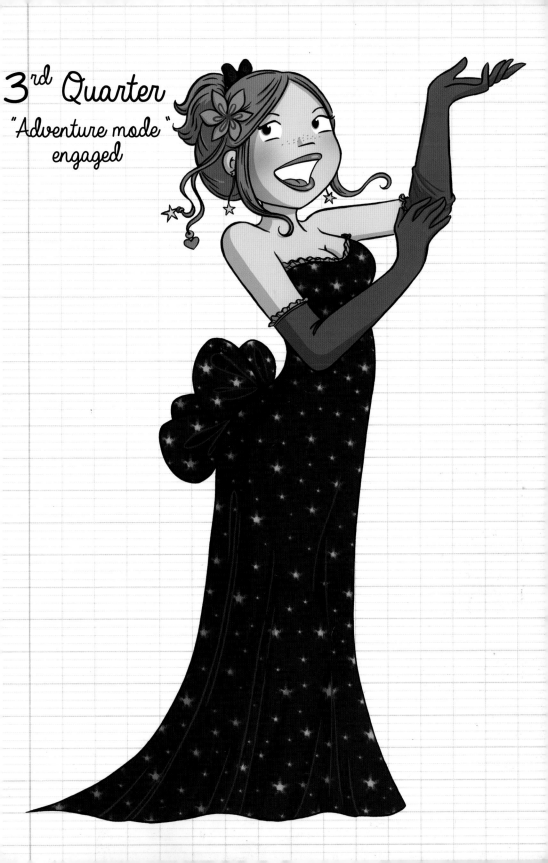

3rd Quarter

"Adventure mode" engaged

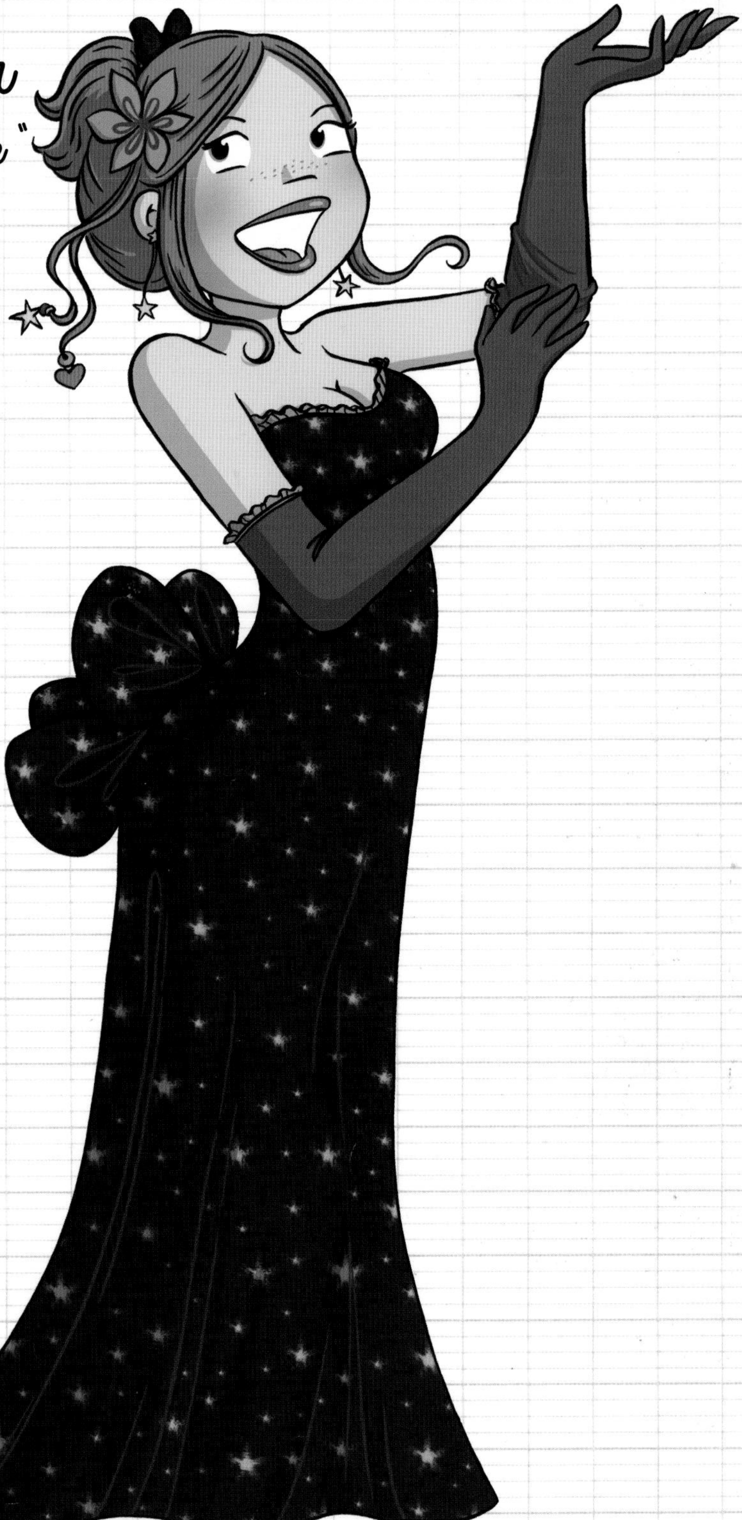

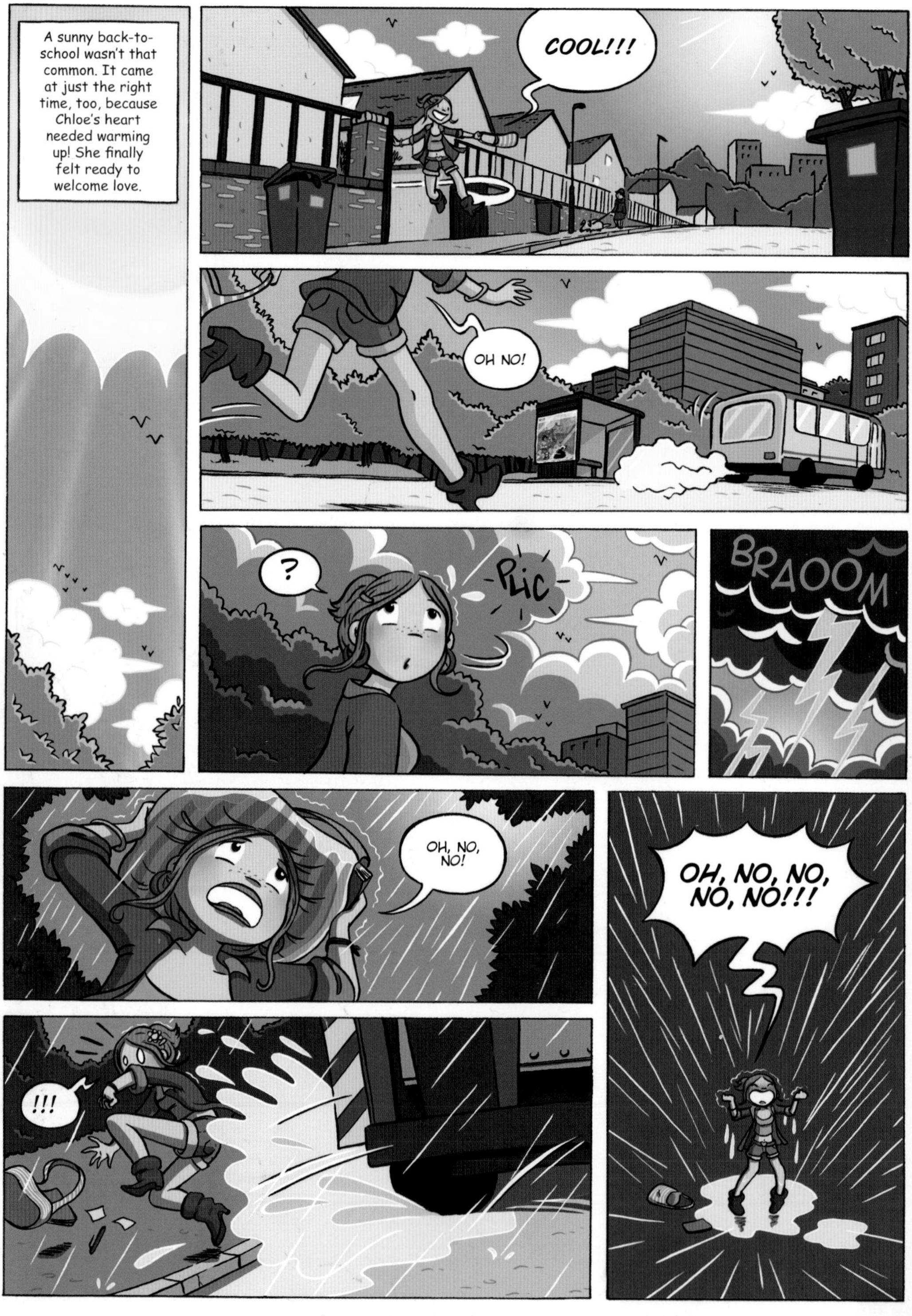
A sunny back-to-school wasn't that common. It came at just the right time, too, because Chloe's heart needed warming up! She finally felt ready to welcome love.
COOL!!!
OH NO!
?
PLIC
BRAOOM
OH, NO, NO!
OH, NO, NO, NO, NO!!!
!!!

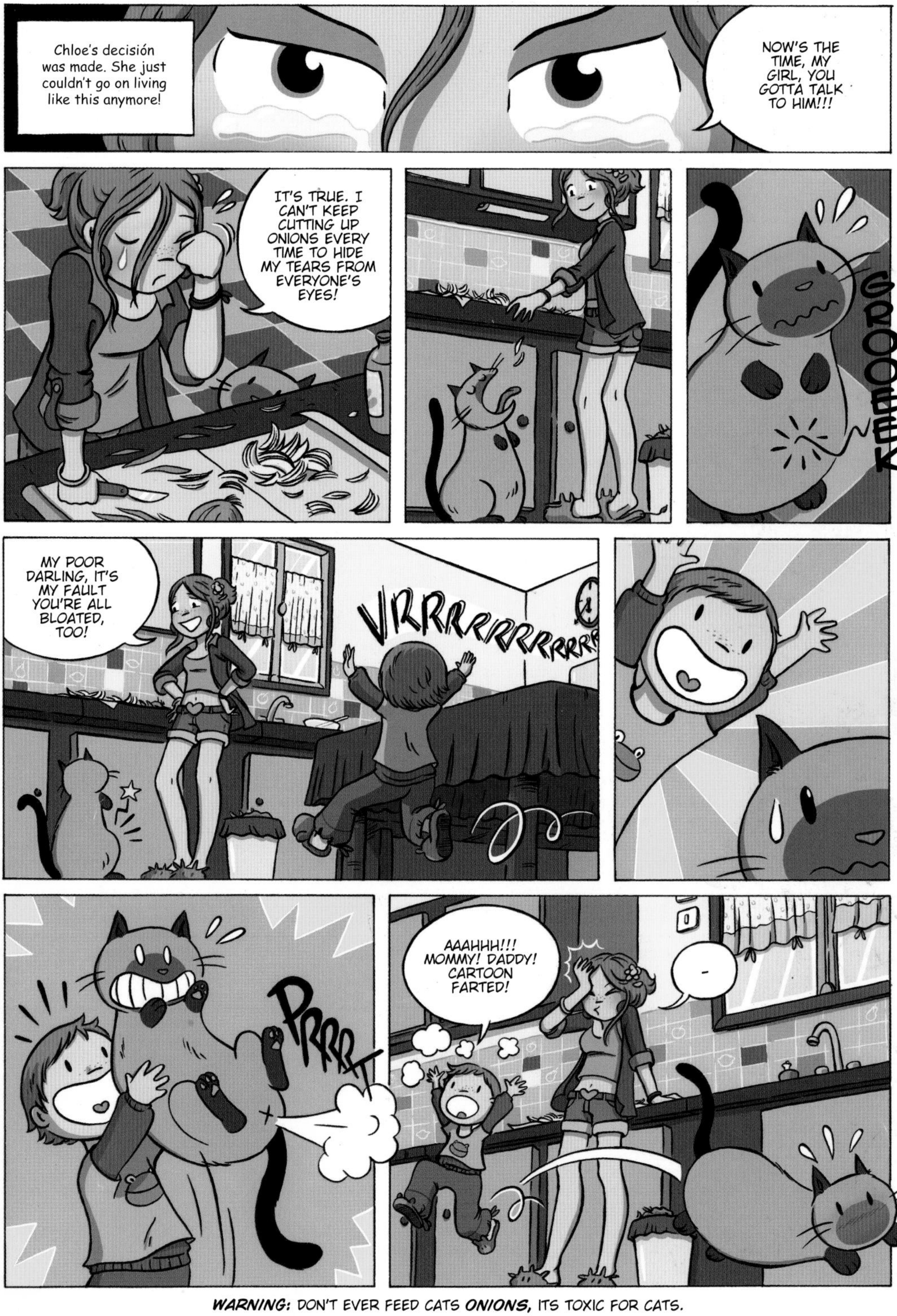
Chloe's decisión was made. She just couldn't go on living like this anymore!
NOW'S THE TIME, MY GIRL, YOU GOTTA TALK TO HIM!!!
IT'S TRUE. I CAN'T KEEP CUTTING UP ONIONS EVERY TIME TO HIDE MY TEARS FROM EVERYONE'S EYES!
GROOEEK
MY POOR DARLING, IT'S MY FAULT YOU'RE ALL BLOATED, TOO!
VRRRRRRRRRRRR
PRRRT
AAAHHH!!! MOMMY! DADDY! CARTOON FARTED!
-

WARNING: DON'T EVER FEED CATS ***ONIONS,*** ITS TOXIC FOR CATS.

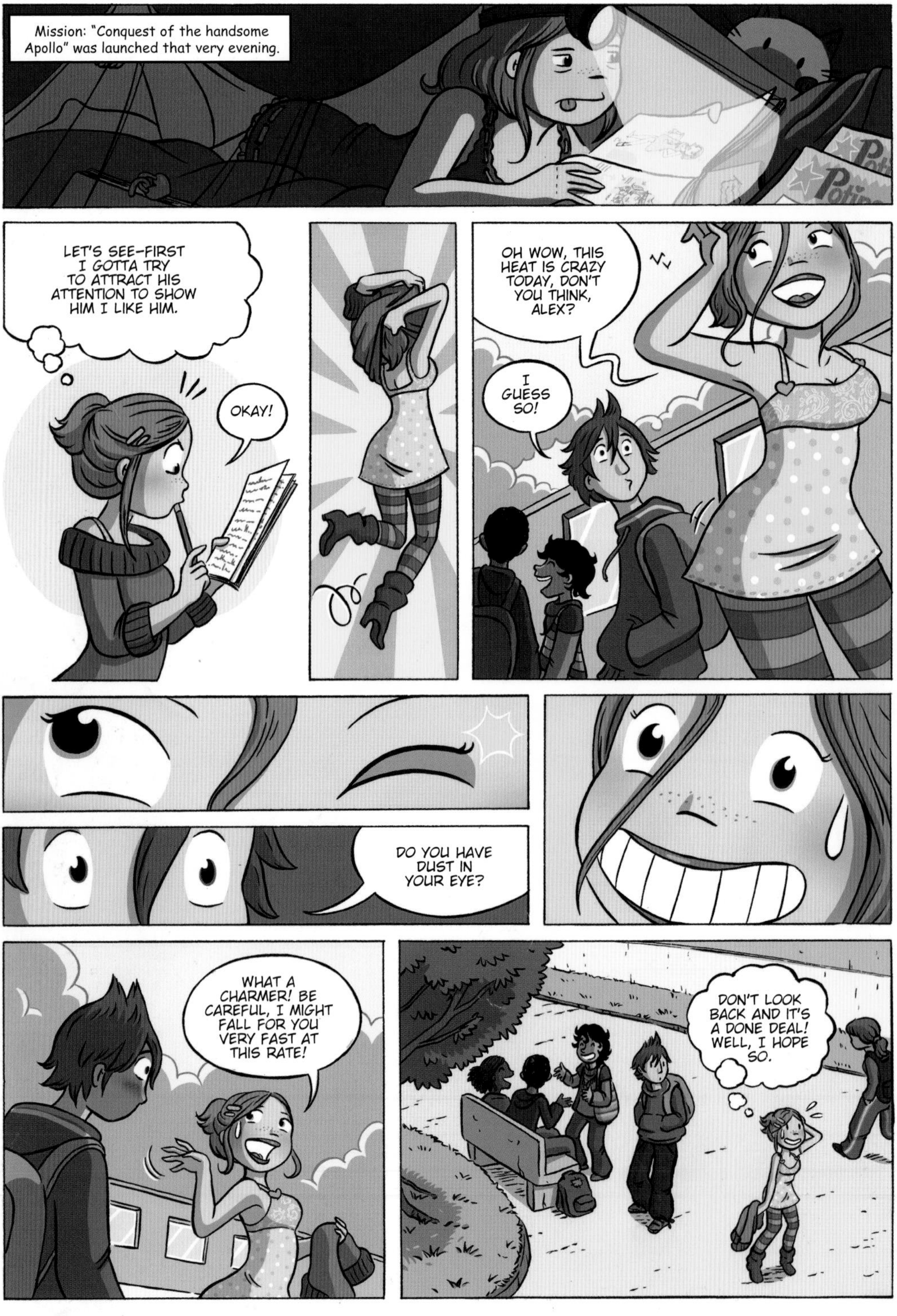

Mission: "Conquest of the handsome Apollo" was launched that very evening.
LET'S SEE–FIRST I GOTTA TRY TO ATTRACT HIS ATTENTION TO SHOW HIM I LIKE HIM.
OKAY!
OH WOW, THIS HEAT IS CRAZY TODAY, DON'T YOU THINK, ALEX?
I GUESS SO!
DO YOU HAVE DUST IN YOUR EYE?
WHAT A CHARMER! BE CAREFUL, I MIGHT FALL FOR YOU VERY FAST AT THIS RATE!
DON'T LOOK BACK AND IT'S A DONE DEAL! WELL, I HOPE SO.

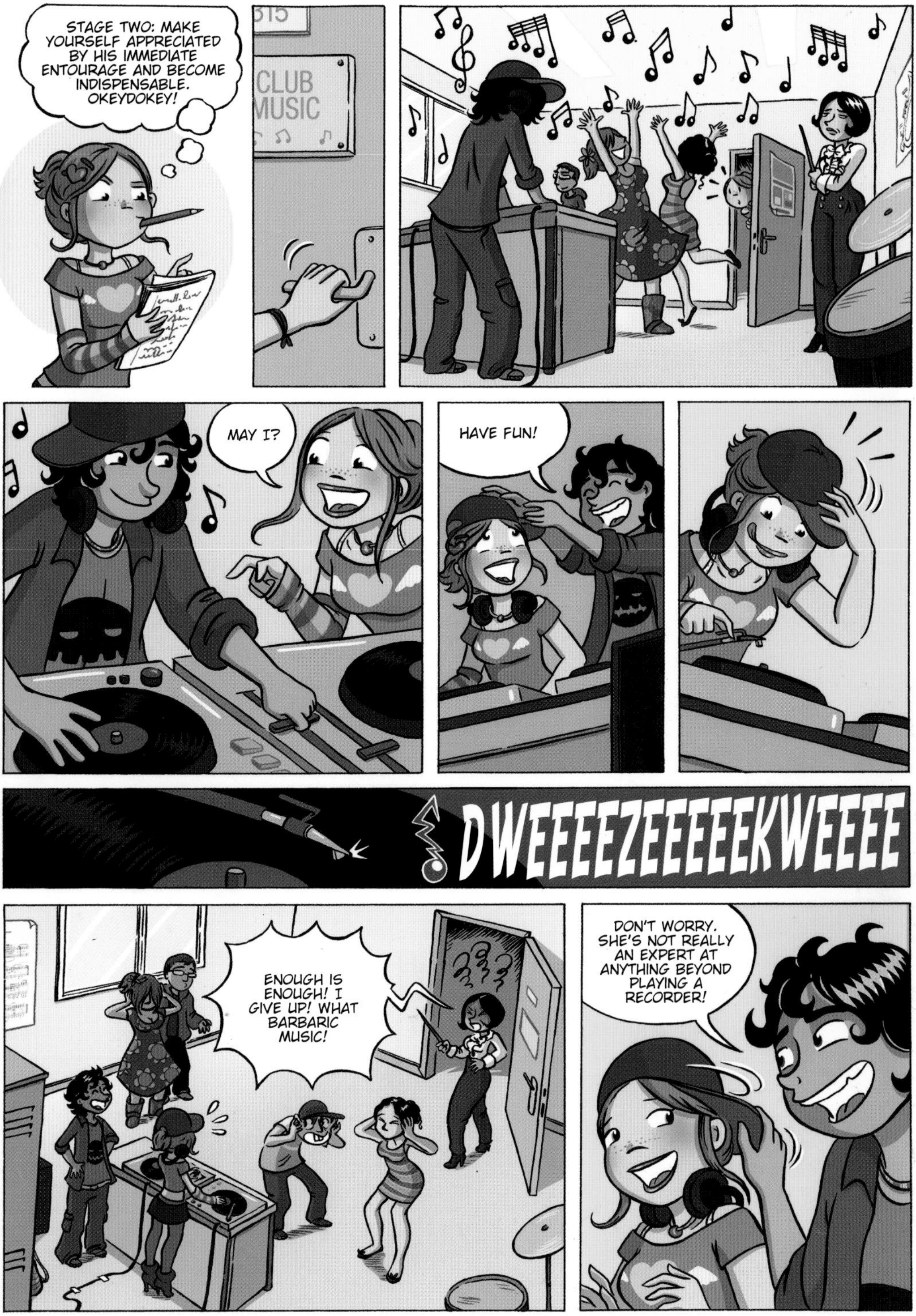
STAGE TWO: MAKE YOURSELF APPRECIATED BY HIS IMMEDIATE ENTOURAGE AND BECOME INDISPENSABLE. OKEYDOKEY!
315
CLUB MUSIC
MAY I?
HAVE FUN!
DWEEEZEEEEEKWEEEE
ENOUGH IS ENOUGH! I GIVE UP! WHAT BARBARIC MUSIC!
DON'T WORRY. SHE'S NOT REALLY AN EXPERT AT ANYTHING BEYOND PLAYING A RECORDER!

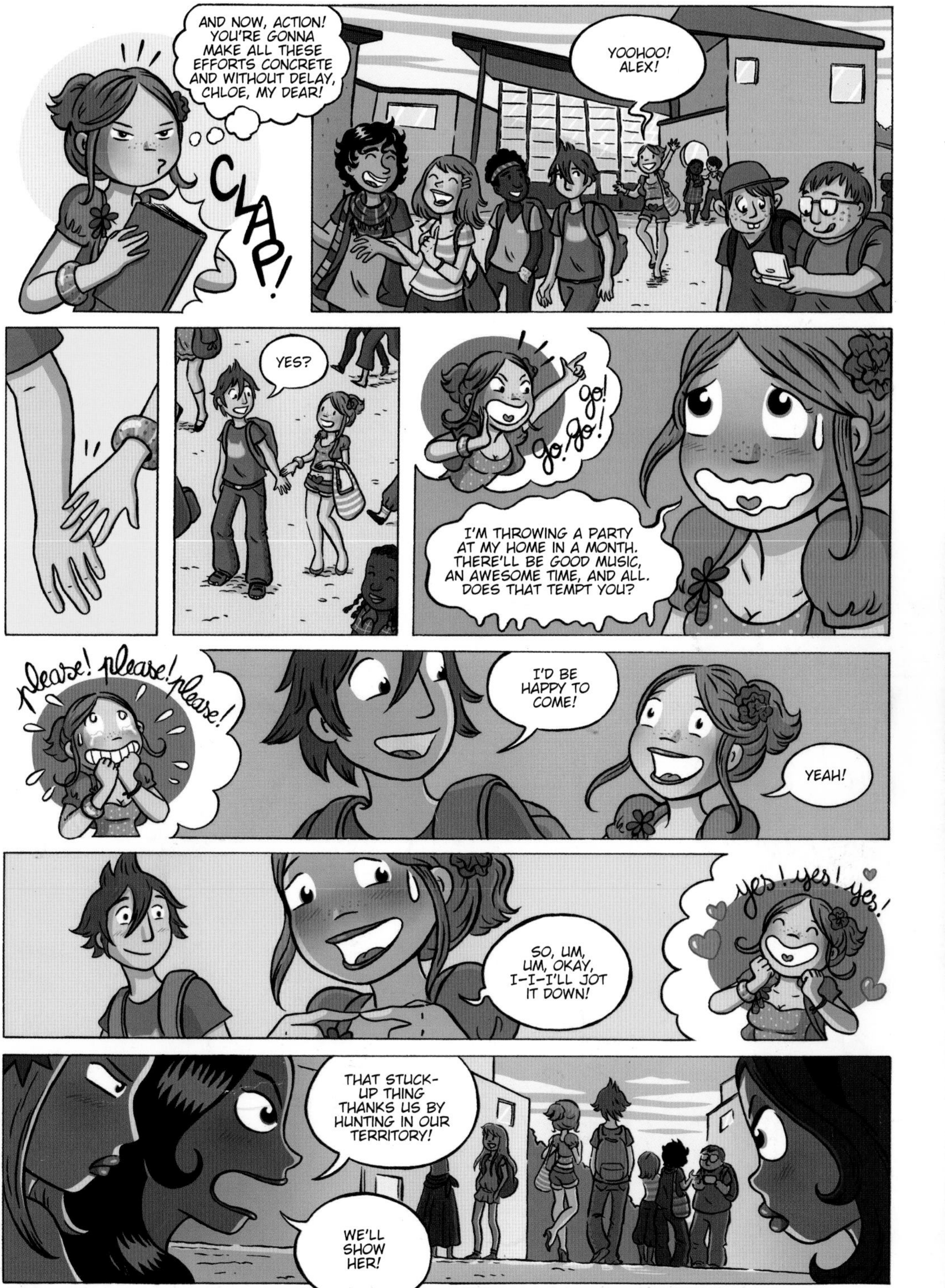
AND NOW, ACTION! YOU'RE GONNA MAKE ALL THESE EFFORTS CONCRETE AND WITHOUT DELAY, CHLOE, MY DEAR!
CLAP!
YOOHOO! ALEX!
YES?
GO! GO! GO!
I'M THROWING A PARTY AT MY HOME IN A MONTH. THERE'LL BE GOOD MUSIC, AN AWESOME TIME, AND ALL. DOES THAT TEMPT YOU?
please! please! please!
I'D BE HAPPY TO COME!
YEAH!
SO, UM, UM, OKAY, I-I-I'LL JOT IT DOWN!
yes! yes! yes!
THAT STUCK-UP THING THANKS US BY HUNTING IN OUR TERRITORY!
WE'LL SHOW HER!

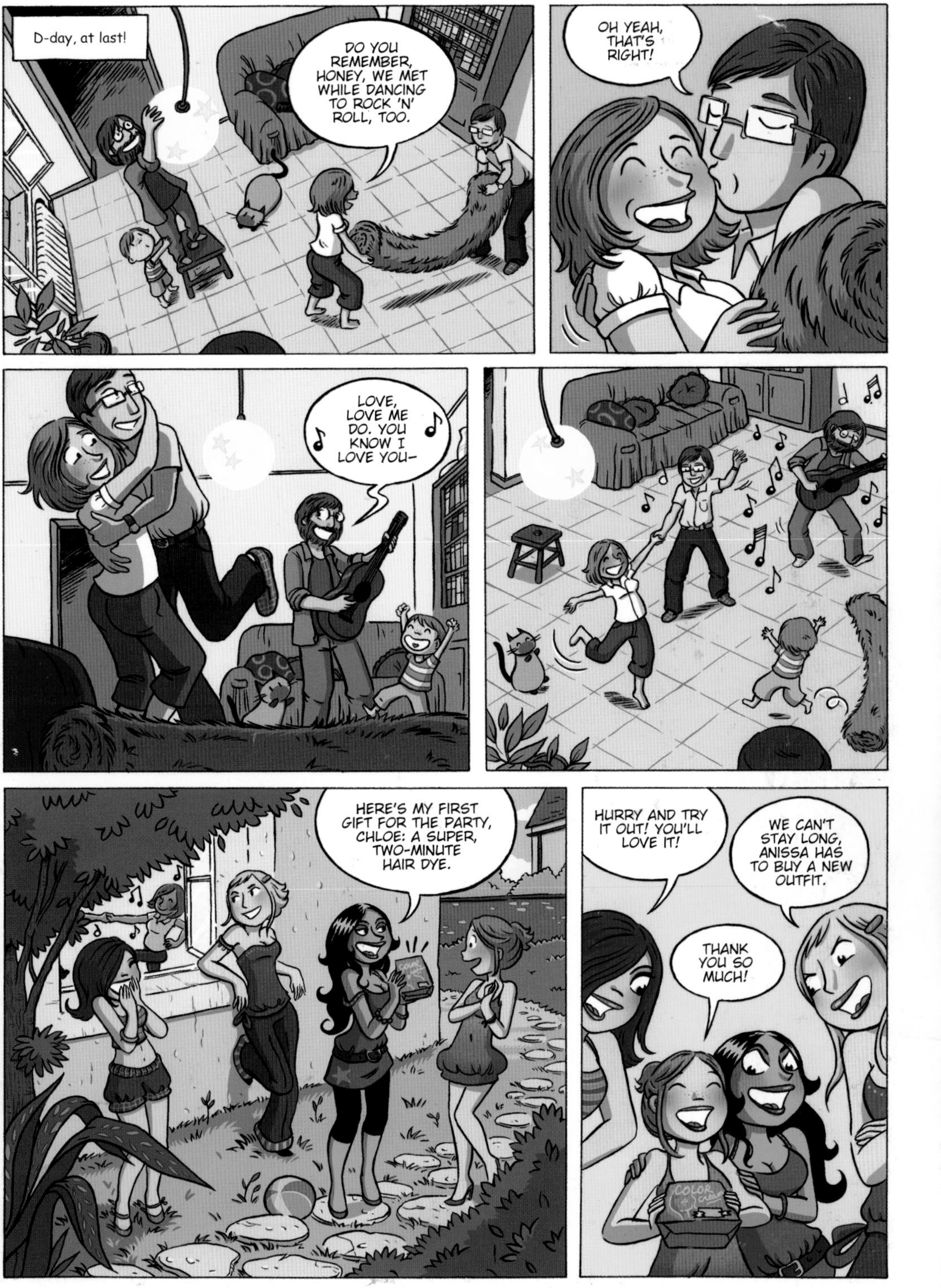
D-day, at last!
DO YOU REMEMBER, HONEY, WE MET WHILE DANCING TO ROCK 'N' ROLL, TOO.
OH YEAH, THAT'S RIGHT!
LOVE, LOVE ME DO. YOU KNOW I LOVE YOU-
HERE'S MY FIRST GIFT FOR THE PARTY, CHLOE: A SUPER, TWO-MINUTE HAIR DYE.
HURRY AND TRY IT OUT! YOU'LL LOVE IT!
WE CAN'T STAY LONG, ANISSA HAS TO BUY A NEW OUTFIT.
THANK YOU SO MUCH!

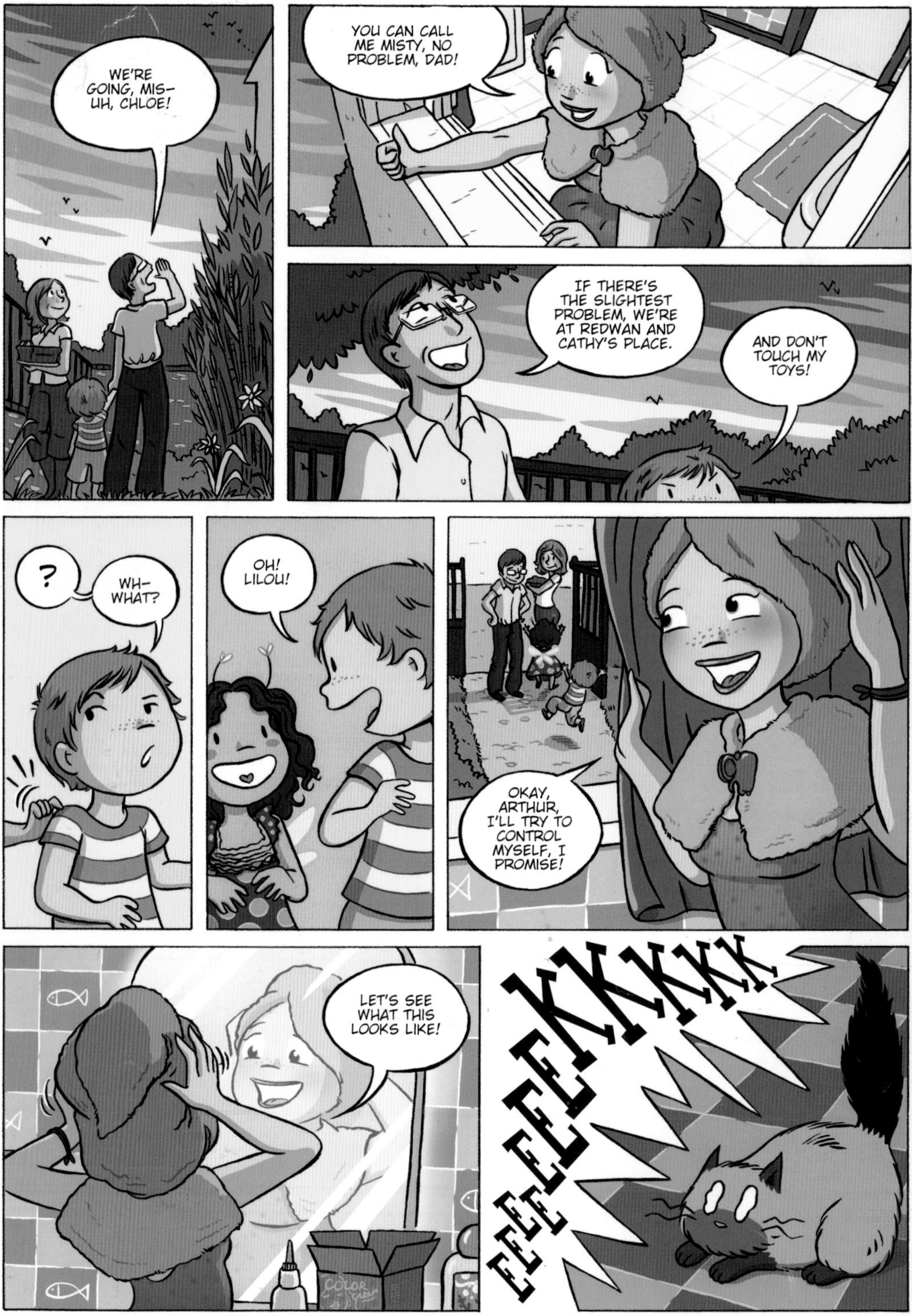
WE'RE GOING, MIS- UH, CHLOE!
YOU CAN CALL ME MISTY, NO PROBLEM, DAD!
IF THERE'S THE SLIGHTEST PROBLEM, WE'RE AT REDWAN AND CATHY'S PLACE.
AND DON'T TOUCH MY TOYS!
?
WH-WHAT?
OH! LILOU!
OKAY, ARTHUR, I'LL TRY TO CONTROL MYSELF, I PROMISE!
LET'S SEE WHAT THIS LOOKS LIKE!
EEEEEEEKKKKK

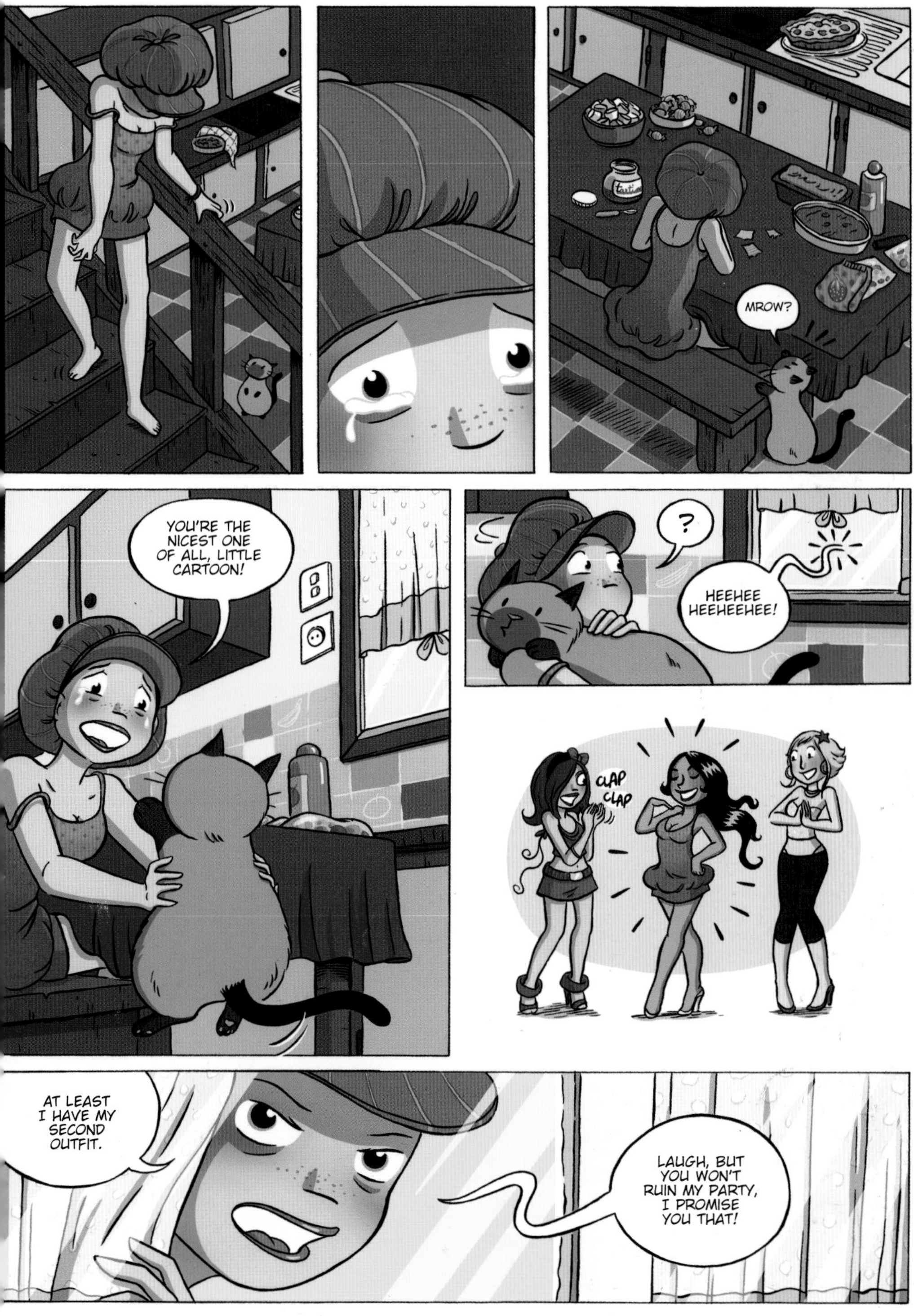

MROW?
YOU'RE THE NICEST ONE OF ALL, LITTLE CARTOON!
?
HEEHEE HEEHEEHEE!
CLAP CLAP
AT LEAST I HAVE MY SECOND OUTFIT.
LAUGH, BUT YOU WON'T RUIN MY PARTY, I PROMISE YOU THAT!

An hour later, the party was in full swing.

But Chloe was still upset.

THEY'RE CERTAINLY NOT GOING TO MONOPOLIZE HIM DURING THE SLOW DANCES.

ALEX, WOULD YOU LIKE TO DANCE WITH ME?

YEAH!

?!

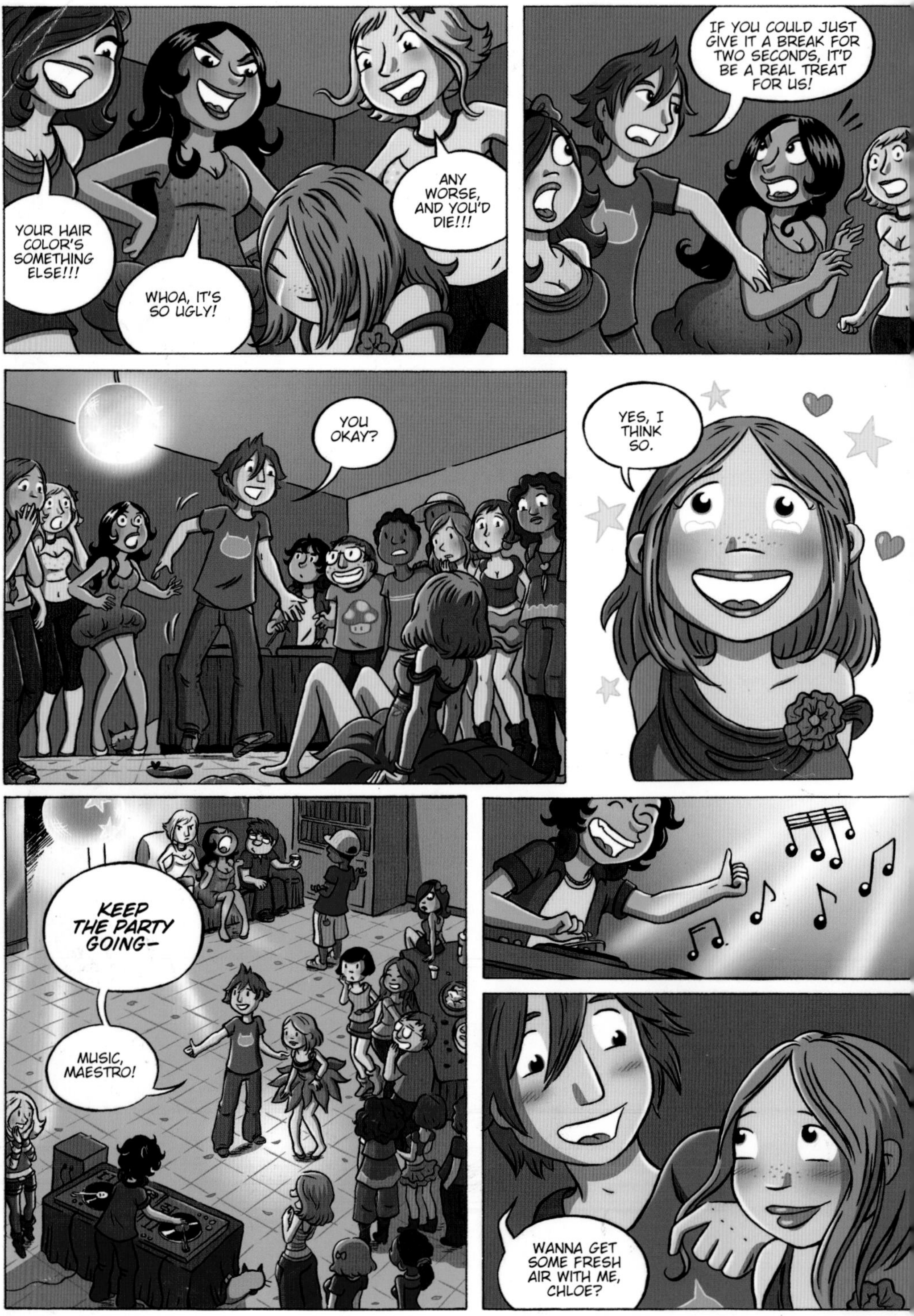
YOUR HAIR COLOR'S SOMETHING ELSE!!!
WHOA, IT'S SO UGLY!
ANY WORSE, AND YOU'D DIE!!!
IF YOU COULD JUST GIVE IT A BREAK FOR TWO SECONDS, IT'D BE A REAL TREAT FOR US!
YOU OKAY?
YES, I THINK SO.
KEEP THE PARTY GOING-
MUSIC, MAESTRO!
WANNA GET SOME FRESH AIR WITH ME, CHLOE?

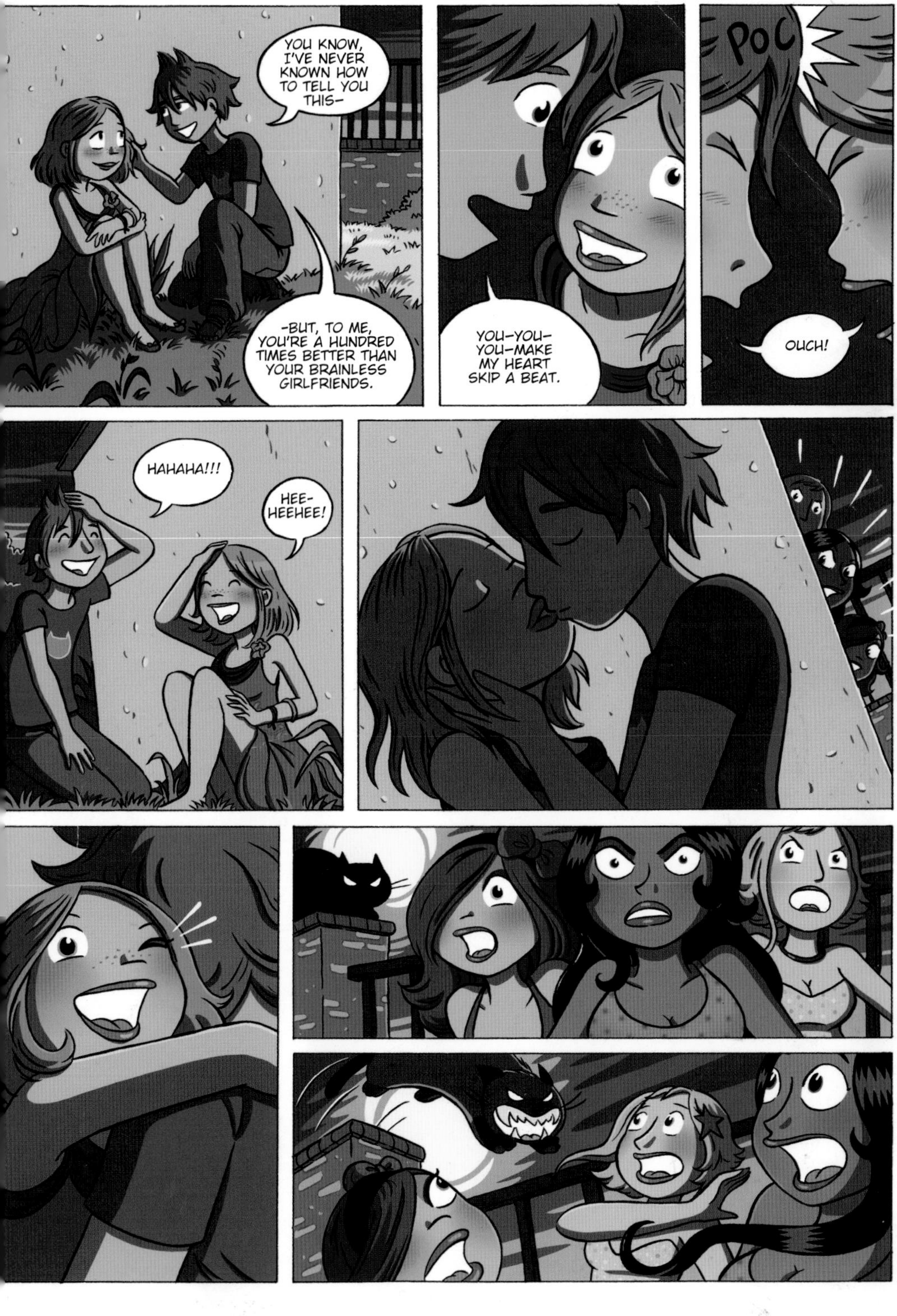
YOU KNOW, I'VE NEVER KNOWN HOW TO TELL YOU THIS–
–BUT, TO ME, YOU'RE A HUNDRED TIMES BETTER THAN YOUR BRAINLESS GIRLFRIENDS.
YOU–YOU–YOU–MAKE MY HEART SKIP A BEAT.
POC
OUCH!
HAHAHA!!!
HEE-HEEHEE!

Report Card
3rd Quarter

BLIN, Chloe, or "Misty,"
for those who love her.
- Eighth Grade, Group C -

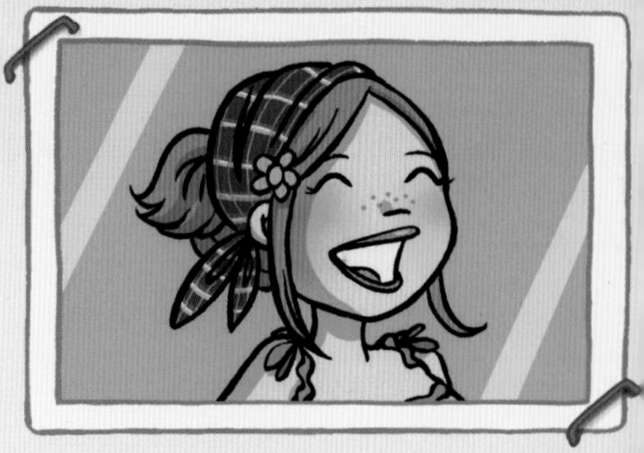

Subjects	Student Grade Averages	Suggestions for Improvement
Appearance	A	You were finally able to silence your critics by creating your own style. Respect!
Self-confidence	A	Smart work. You succeeded in asserting your choices amid adversity.
Observation Skills	B	You didn't rest on your laurels. Good consistency. Bravo!
Attractiveness	B	Real involvement The whole package has become very satisfying.
Popularity	A	Congratulations. You finally understood that popularity wasn't very important if it doesn't come from the people you love.
Average for This Period	A	

General Comments:
All the readers would like to pay tribute to Chloe's tenacity. She was able to take charge of herself and adapt at her own rhythm without ever giving up. 9th grade holds a lot of promise.

Notification: this grade report is the original copy and must be preserved,

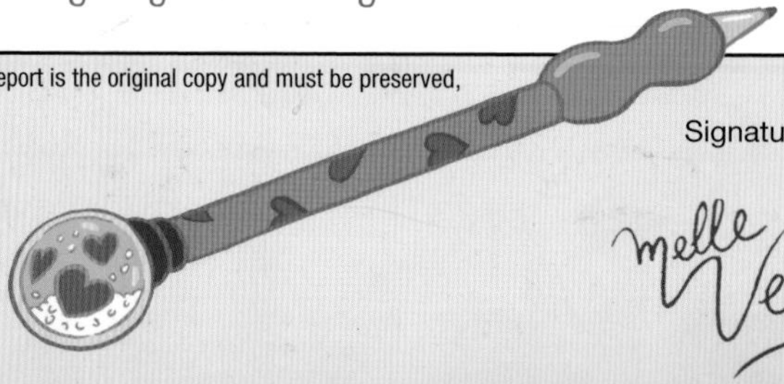

Signature of the home room teacher:

Melle Vernier

- Georges Brassens Middle School - Georges Brassens Middle School -

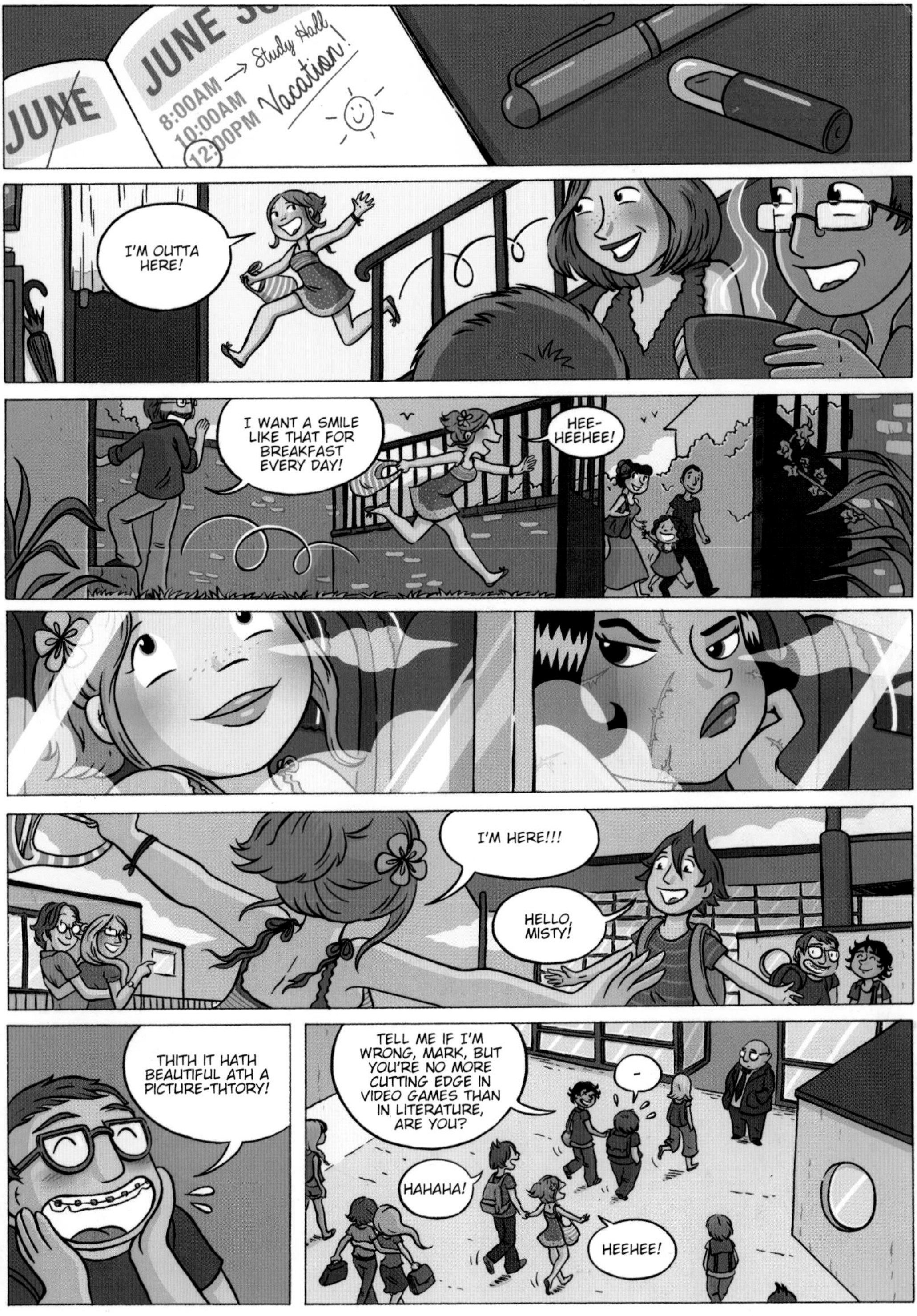
JUNE
JUNE 30
8:00AM → Study Hall
10:00AM
12:00PM Vacation!
I'M OUTTA HERE!
I WANT A SMILE LIKE THAT FOR BREAKFAST EVERY DAY!
HEE-HEEHEE!
I'M HERE!!!
HELLO, MISTY!
THITH IT HATH BEAUTIFUL ATH A PICTURE-THTORY!
TELL ME IF I'M WRONG, MARK, BUT YOU'RE NO MORE CUTTING EDGE IN VIDEO GAMES THAN IN LITERATURE, ARE YOU?
-
HAHAHA!
HEEHEE!

Kisses and Shells

Wandering

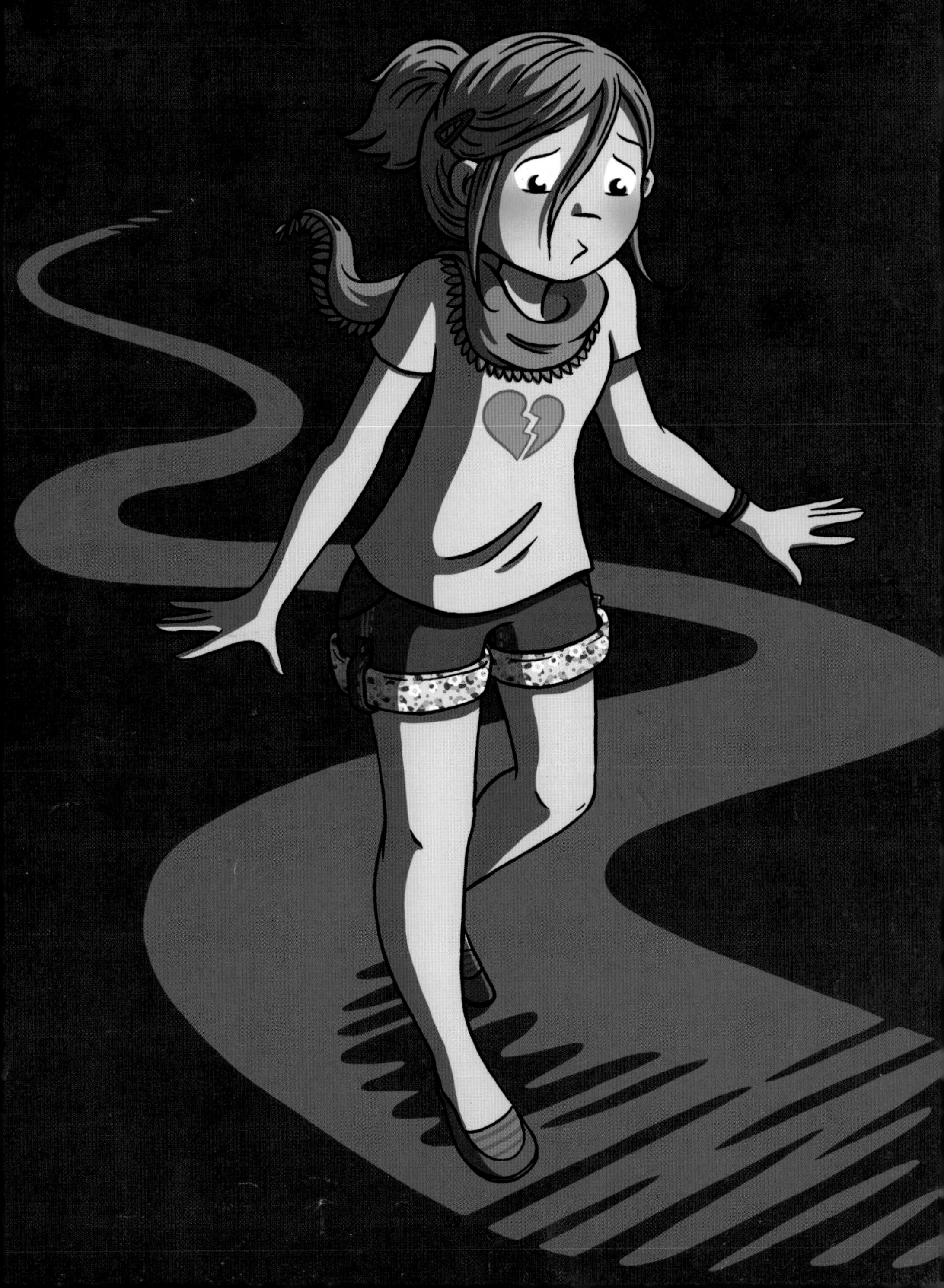

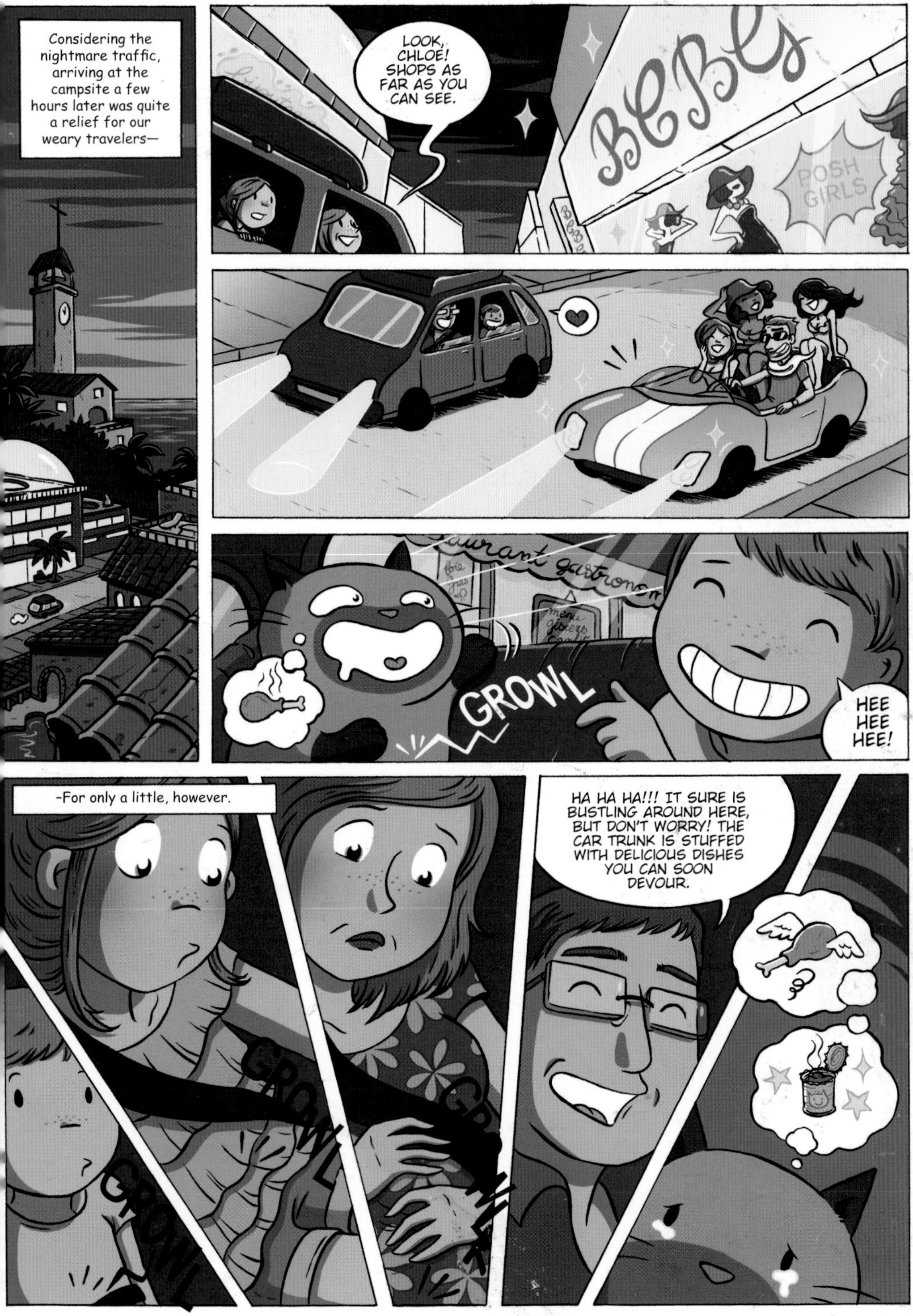
Considering the nightmare traffic, arriving at the campsite a few hours later was quite a relief for our weary travelers—
LOOK, CHLOE! SHOPS AS FAR AS YOU CAN SEE.
BEBEs
POSH GIRLS
GROWL
HEE HEE HEE!
-For only a little, however.
HA HA HA!!! IT SURE IS BUSTLING AROUND HERE, BUT DON'T WORRY! THE CAR TRUNK IS STUFFED WITH DELICIOUS DISHES YOU CAN SOON DEVOUR.
GROWL
GROWL
GROWL
GROWL

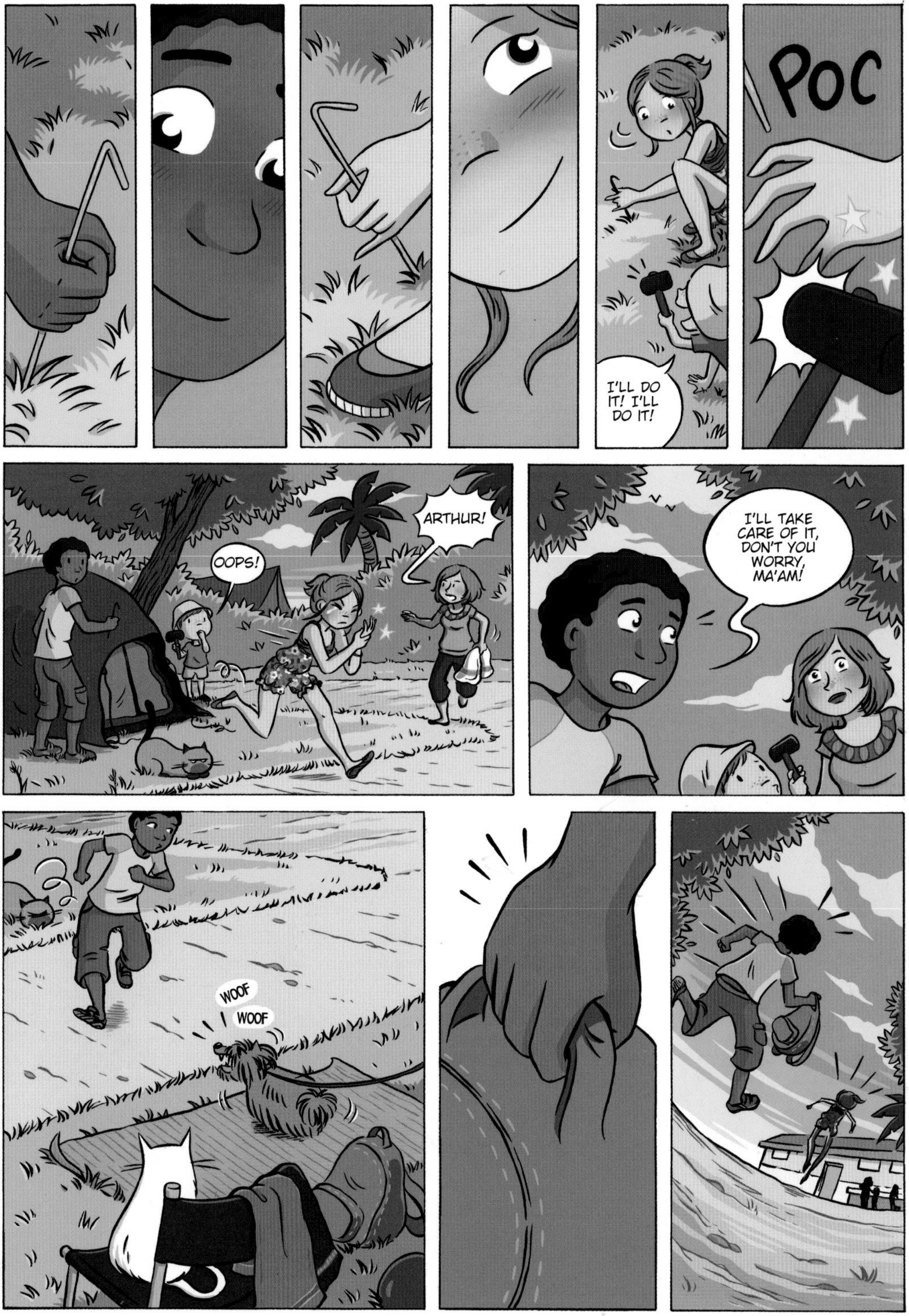

I'LL DO IT! I'LL DO IT!
POC
OOPS!
ARTHUR!
I'LL TAKE CARE OF IT, DON'T YOU WORRY, MA'AM!
WOOF
WOOF

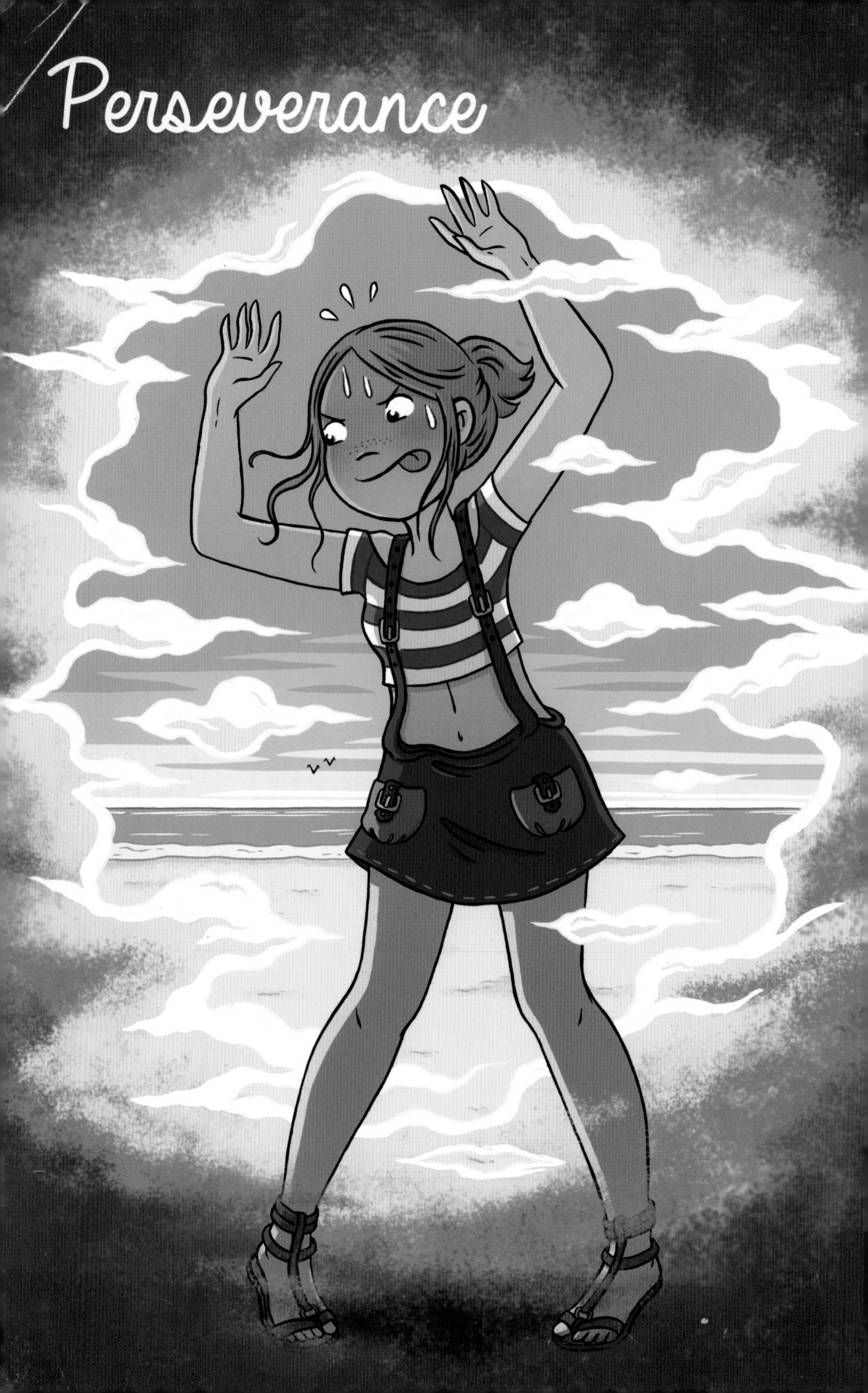
Perseverance

The Obvious

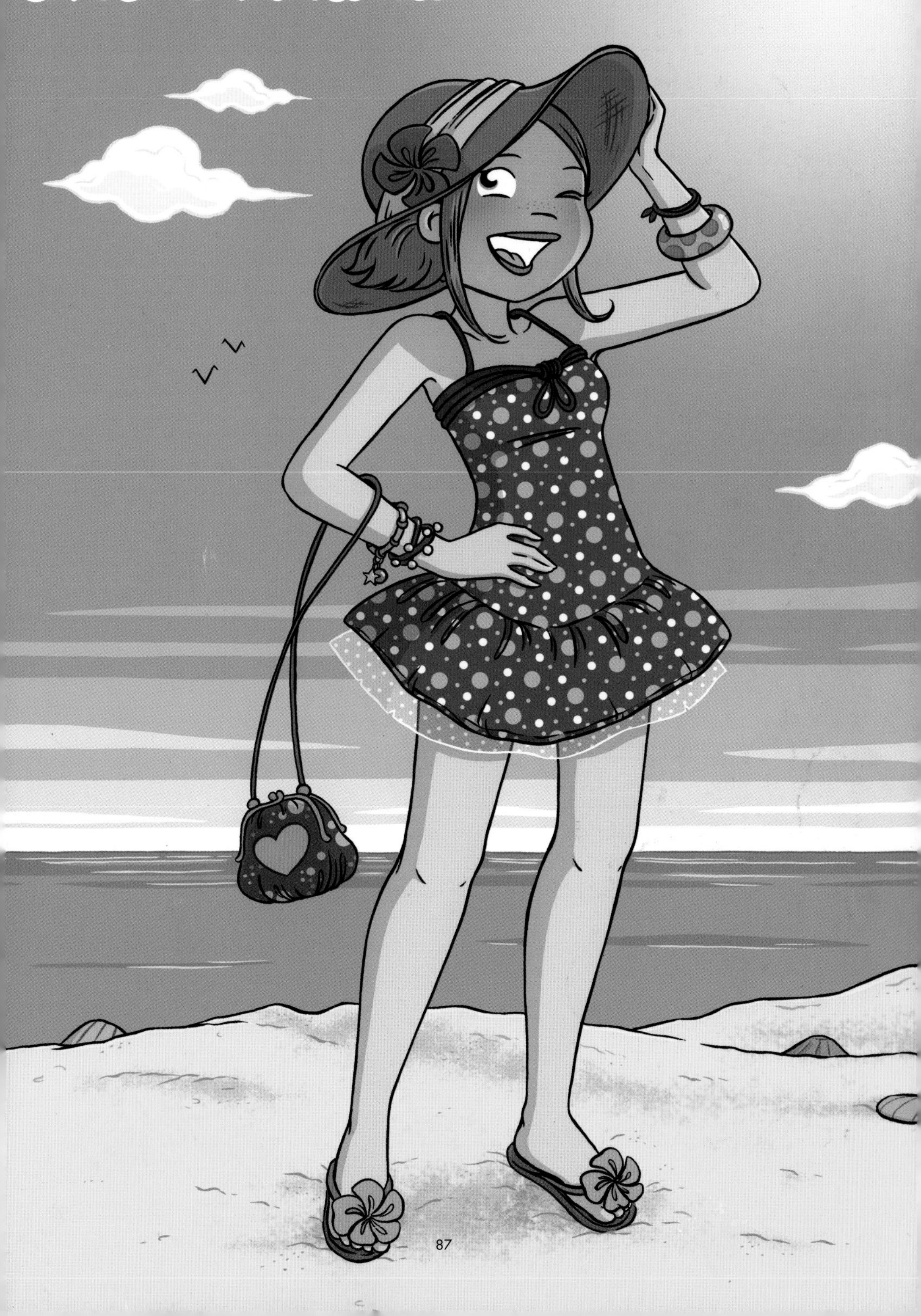

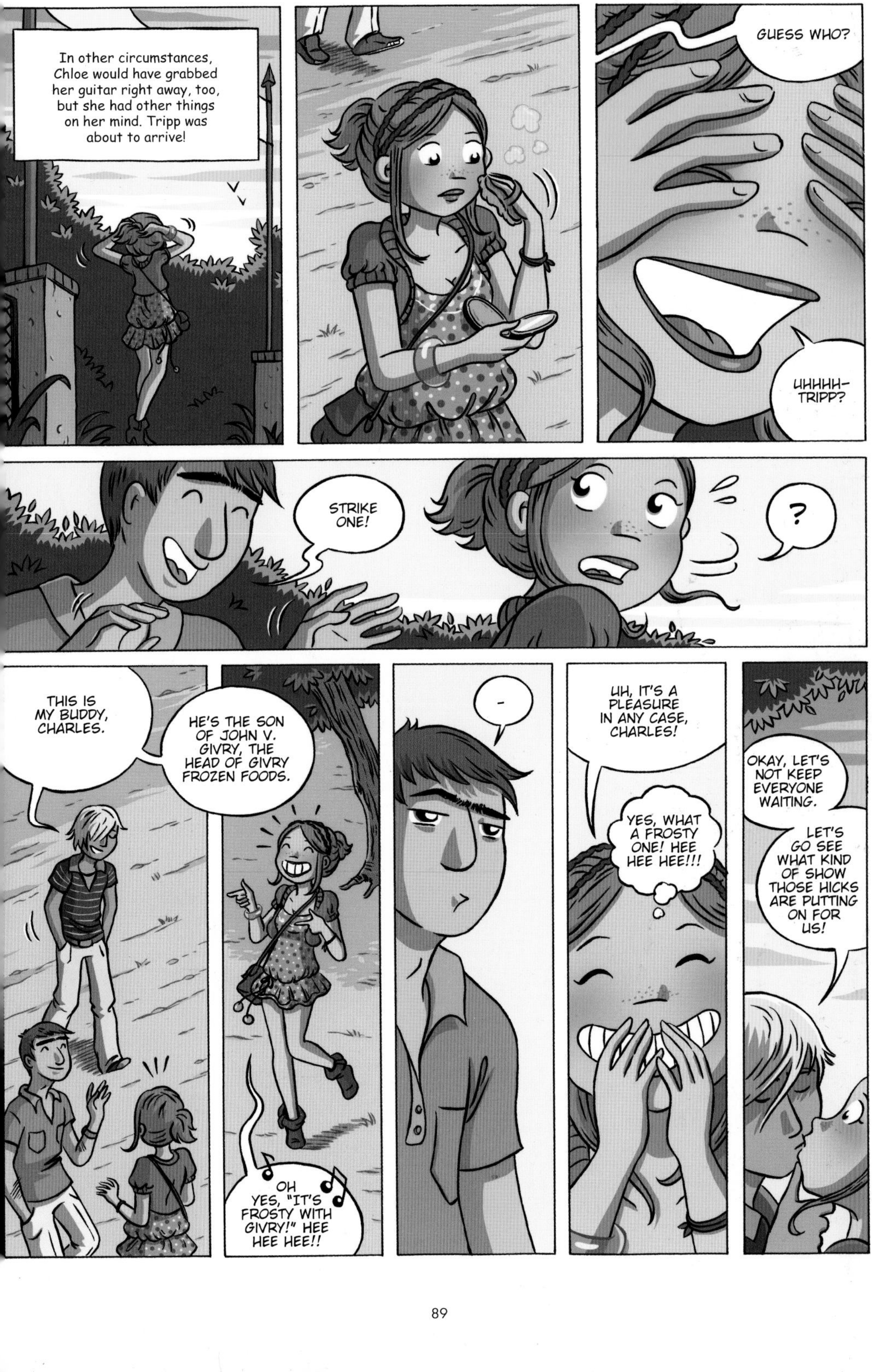
In other circumstances, Chloe would have grabbed her guitar right away, too, but she had other things on her mind. Tripp was about to arrive!
GUESS WHO?
UHHHH-TRIPP?
STRIKE ONE!
?
THIS IS MY BUDDY, CHARLES.
HE'S THE SON OF JOHN V. GIVRY, THE HEAD OF GIVRY FROZEN FOODS.
OH YES, "IT'S FROSTY WITH GIVRY!" HEE HEE HEE!!
-
UH, IT'S A PLEASURE IN ANY CASE, CHARLES!
YES, WHAT A FROSTY ONE! HEE HEE HEE!!!
OKAY, LET'S NOT KEEP EVERYONE WAITING.
LET'S GO SEE WHAT KIND OF SHOW THOSE HICKS ARE PUTTING ON FOR US!

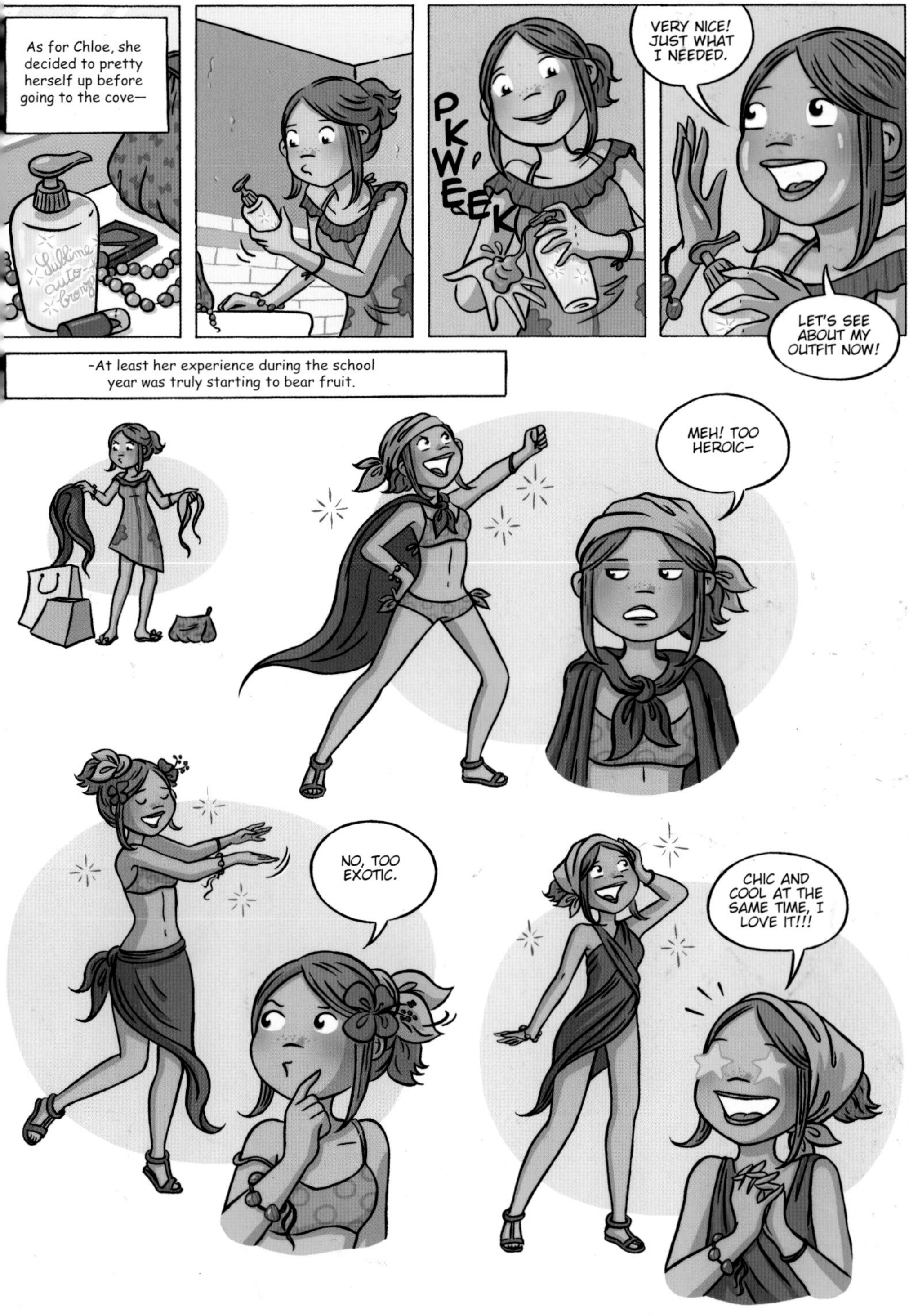
As for Chloe, she decided to pretty herself up before going to the cove—
Sublime auto-bronze
PKWEEEK
VERY NICE! JUST WHAT I NEEDED.
LET'S SEE ABOUT MY OUTFIT NOW!
-At least her experience during the school year was truly starting to bear fruit.
MEH! TOO HEROIC-
NO, TOO EXOTIC.
CHIC AND COOL AT THE SAME TIME, I LOVE IT!!!

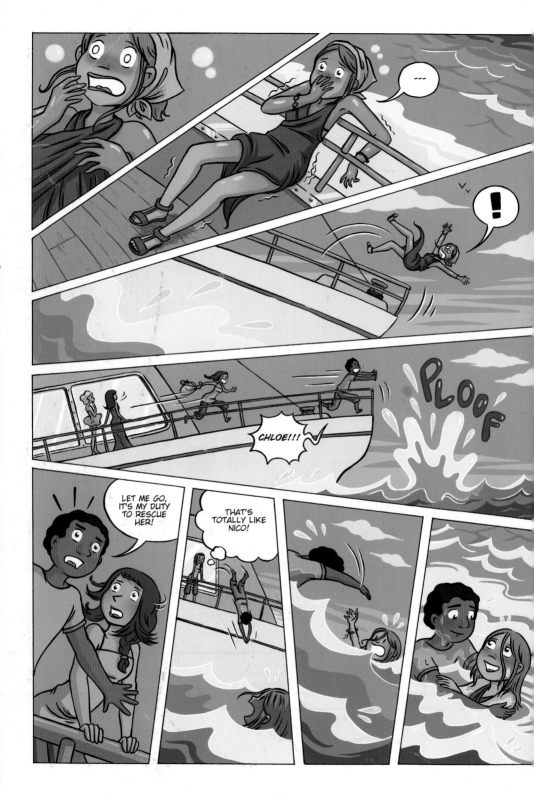

However, right in the middle of the August 15th fireworks, something incredible happened.

THE END

GLASGOW, SCOTLAND. CLYDE ACADEMY.

CAN'T LIE.

THERE ARE SOME THINGS I'LL MISS ABOUT CLYDE ACADEMY.

LIKE THIS *DELIGHTFUL* LUNCH FOOD.

OR STARING AT THE BACK OF RYAN CLEGG'S... NECK.

THERE ARE ALSO THINGS I WILL *NOT* MISS:

LIKE MATH TESTS AND---

KIRSTY McRAE!

SHE AND HER FRIENDS DRIVE ME CRAZY!

EXCUSE ME, CHERRY COSTELLO!

WE NEED SOME MORE ROOM.

WAP

HEY, GIRLS!

DID YOU KNOW, CHERRY'S MUM THOUGHT SHE WAS SUCH A *LOSER* THAT SHE DITCHED HER AND RAN OFF TO LIVE ON THE OTHER SIDE OF THE WORLD?

YOU DON'T KNOW ANYTHING ABOUT MY MUM!

Don't miss the full story in SWEETIES #1 "Cherry/Skye," available at booksellers everywhere!

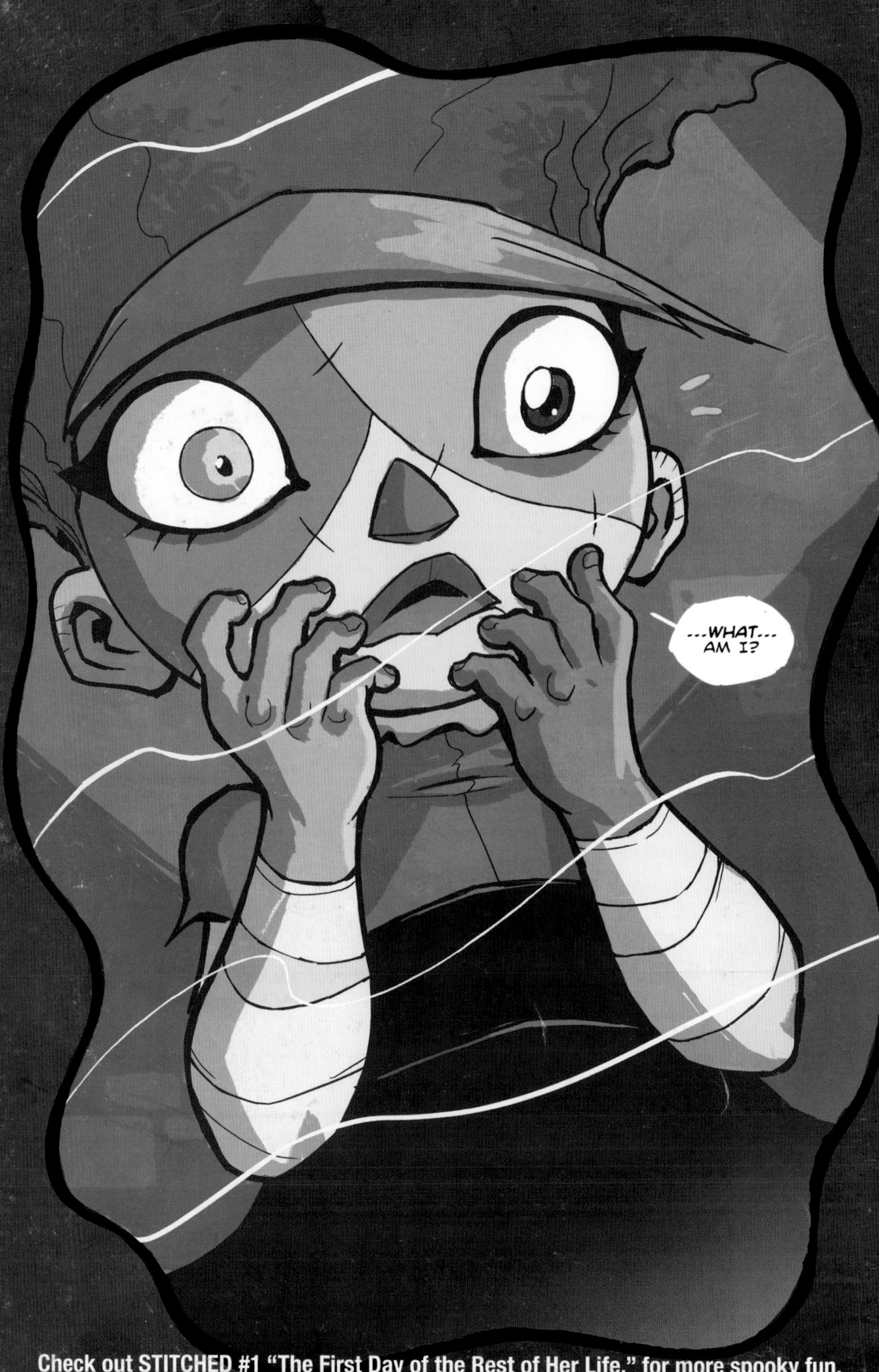
...WHAT... AM I?

Welcome to Charmz

I am definitely obsessed with all things romance. It's fun, it's dramatic, and it's all about love. I think love is pretty amazing, don't you? When your heart beats faster at the sound of someone else's voice or the way they smile, you just feel more alive. And terrified! Or how about when just being around that special someone makes you feel like you're flying? Like you could do anything? Falling in love is one of the most incredible feelings, ever.

Of course, love is also complicated and painful sometimes. They don't call them "crushes" for nothing!

Yet, when I'm feeling kind of meh or sad, the first thing I want to do is read a romance. Maybe it's because everyone falls in love, has heartbreak and heartache. Maybe it's because there's really nothing like your first kiss. Whatever the reason, when I want to feel better, I pick up a romance and settle in. Usually with tea and chocolate, if I'm being totally honest.

Which brings us to Charmz, a new line of graphic novels just for you! With stories from all over the world, Charmz wants to celebrate love. Whether we're hanging out in Somerset, UK, the wilds of France, speeding through space, or waking up in a cemetery, love finds our characters and digs right in.

Whether you're in the mood for a (literally!) sweet tale about sisters, chocolate, and forbidden love, or exploring the mysterious darkness of Assumption Cemetery where vampires and swamp boys romance stitched girls, you'll find a lot to relate to.

My favorite kinds of romance are epic, sweeping, and probably just a little bit hilarious. As seriously as I take love, if you don't laugh a little at the things we'll do for it, well, you'll end up actually lovesick. Which is definitely something the girls in our books have to deal with from time to time. Not to mention fashion faux pas, weird chocolate recipes, ghosts, zombie sheep, and puzzles through time and space!

I've read a lot of romances and I definitely have my favorites. I think the one I would take on a desert island would have to be *Pride and Prejudice* by Jane Austen. I know, it's old, but it's so witty, and funny, and real. It's been adapted so many times but it always feels fresh and relevant. Anyone could be those characters. Me. You.

Aside from editing this line of graphic novels, I'm also writing one: STITCHED. This spooky little cemetery book with vampires, werewolves, swamp boys and stitched girls is very dear to me. It's the book I've always wanted to write, with spectacularly weird creatures, spooky adventures, and lots and lots of awkward, splendid, romance. Crimson Volania Mulch is my favorite kind of girl; complicated, smart, curious, kind…but a little bit preoccupied with her own problems. And way too judgmental. No one is perfect! And if I woke up only knowing my name in a strange place, I might be a little self-involved, too. I mean, just who is that pretty boy she meets on her first night "alive," and where is her mother? What does a badger/hedgehog actually eat? Do werewolves like cupcakes?

What I want Charmz to be for you is like the book equivalent of a hot chocolate; sweet, maybe a little dark sometimes, comforting, and made just for you. You can curl up with our tales, settle in, and enjoy falling in love with our characters just like they fall in love with each other.

Remember: stories matter, love is powerful, and there's nothing like a love story to make you feel alive.

–Mariah McCourt

Please write to me any time about Charmz! mariah@papercutz.com

I would love hear from you.

STAY IN TOUCH!

EMAIL:	charmz@papercutz
WEB:	www.papercutz.com
TWITTER:	@papercutzgn
FACEBOOK:	PAPERCUTZGRAPHICNOVELS
REGULAR MAIL:	Charmz, 160 Broadway, Suite 700, East Wing, New York, NY 10038

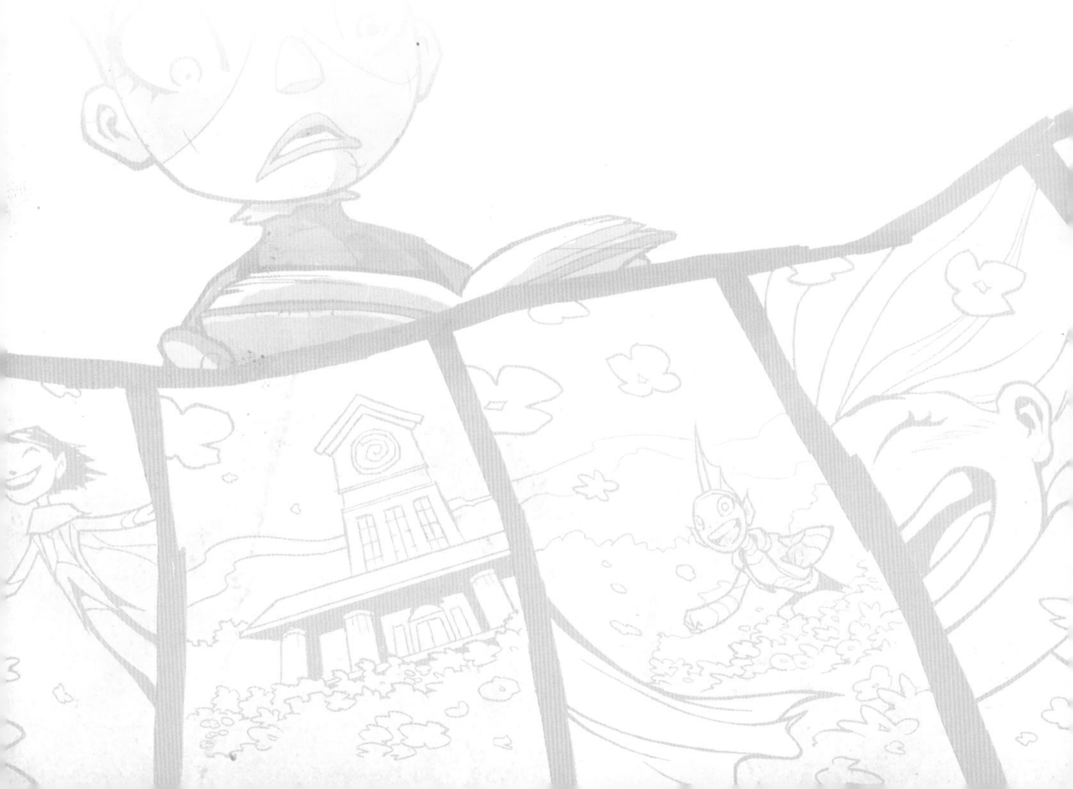